'I'm pregnant!'

It was Brian's misfortune to have taken a drink just as she made her announcement. His face immediately turned purple and he coughed violently.

'You're—you're sure?' he wheezed.

She straightened up. 'Sure I'm pregnant or sure it's yours?'

He ignored her frosty tone. 'Of course it's mine. I'm just asking if you'd seen a doctor for confirmation.'

'I *am* a doctor. There are no financial worries, but I would like the baby to know his or her father.' She looked at him, wary of what he'd say.

'I'm going to be a dad. Gail.' He waited until she looked back at him. 'We're going to be fine.' Then he waited for her to inform him that she could do fine on her own, thank you very much.

She surprised him by smiling.

'Maybe we will at that.'

Dear Reader,

A warm welcome to Special Edition.

Considering Kate, a new STANISLASKI novel by number one *New York Times* bestselling author Nora Roberts, is our first book this month and also available from mid-July is the linked book, *The Stanislaski Sisters*, which contains Kate's mother's story.

Our popular THAT'S MY BABY! mini-series continues with *My Little One* by Linda Randall Wisdom. See how this marriage-of-convenience-for-the-sake-of-the-baby story turns out. Talking of children, look out for the first book in a new trilogy from wonderful author Laurie Paige. *Something To Talk About* begins THE WINDRAVEN LEGACY where newly-discovered secrets threaten to shatter the lives and loves of this family. The second book, *When I See Your Face*, is out in July.

The third of the MONTANA BRIDES linked books—*Just Pretending* by Myrna Mackenzie—storms onto the shelves this month. Along with five orphaned children, including nine-month-old triplets, in *Mother in a Moment* by Allison Leigh and a passionate lone wolf in *Gray Wolf's Woman* by Peggy Webb.

Enjoy!

The Editors

My Little One

LINDA RANDALL WISDOM

SILHOUETTE®
SPECIAL EDITION™

*All the characters in this book have no existence outside the imagination
of the author, and have no relation whatsoever to anyone bearing the
same name or names. They are not even distantly inspired by any
individual known or unknown to the author, and all the incidents are
pure invention.*

*First published in Great Britain 2002
Silhouette Books, Eton House, 18-24 Paradise Road,
Richmond, Surrey TW9 1SR*

© Words by Wisdom 2000

ISBN 0 373 16831 4

23-0602

*Printed and bound in Spain
by Litografia Rosés S.A., Barcelona*

In remembrance of my dad, Robert Randall

An equal-opportunity dad who taught me to bait my own hook and bought me dolls. Who let me hang out at the airplane hangars and took me to Sunday school. Who told me I could be anything I wanted to be and told everyone about his daughter, the romance writer.

I miss you so much, Dad.

LINDA RANDALL WISDOM

sold her first two novels to Silhouette Romance in 1979, fittingly on her tenth wedding anniversary. When people ask her husband what it's like to be married to a romance writer, he tells them it isn't boring! Linda and her husband live in Southern California in an area close enough to go to the beach or the mountains, depending on their mood. They have two dogs, Bogie, a terrier/Chihuahua; Fergie, a Saint Bernard/Lab who's confident the world revolves around her; four parrots and a desert tortoise.

Dear Reader,

I guess most readers expect a mum to write the expectant mum and kids books. Yes, I'm a mum, but my kids have fur and four feet and feathers and claws. And while some of them have appeared in some of my books, they aren't exactly the same as human kids, are they? Maybe I'm not a mum of human kids, but as someone who's never grown up, it's easy to understand them.

Kids are great. They can be painfully honest, they enjoy the least little thing and they can laugh and have fun like no one else can. And, if you're a kid at heart, they'll let you join in.

For good examples of mums, I have my own mum and friends to use, and my dad was a wonderful example of what a dad should be.

I observe and ask questions, talk to mums and pick their minds. And then I put my own spin on it. There are times when fiction is safer than the truth.

I hope my readers have enjoyed all the kids I've written about in the past and the ones to come. Because I don't plan to ever grow up!

Linda Randall Wisdom

Prologue

"Do you know in the past three months I haven't met one man I've wanted to date? Was there an epidemic wiping out all the presentable men, and no one told me about it?"

"What are you complaining about, Barbara? At least you're around men all day." The woman saying this breathed a soft sigh as she settled in the hot bubbling mineral pool. "There's so much estrogen in our office none of us will ever need hormone replacement therapy."

"Cute, Rita, really cute." The answering drawl was filled with sarcasm. "Yes, I am around men most of the day. Men everywhere. Men who can't escape my charm even if I want them to. And why? Because they are *in jail!*"

"They're not all guilty, are they?" A soft-spoken blonde frowned as she inspected her manicure. "Didn't you say that cute stockbroker who stole from his clients was in jail because he couldn't make bail? I heard him say on the news that he didn't do it."

"Right, Cheryl, someone else opened that account in the Cayman Islands just so they could frame him," one other woman said.

"It's been done before," Cheryl insisted.

The group just rolled their eyes.

"Barbara's wrong. There are some presentable men around. In fact, I know of two men who are perfect date material."

"Then why are you in here on a Friday night instead of out there with one of them?" Lucie challenged.

"Because they're not perfect for me." She sunk down until the water bubbled up around her shoulders. "How about a good-looking computer consultant who enjoys viewing obscure art as much as you do? He has a sail-boat he takes out on the weekends, skis and can even cook."

"If you haven't latched on to him, something has to be wrong," Barbara said, naturally suspicious.

"There's not. We tried dating, but we weren't more than ten minutes into our date when we realized we would be better friends than lovers," she said ruefully. "His biological clock is on overtime while I keep slap-ping the snooze alarm on mine. But he's been saying just what we're saying. In his case, he's having trouble meeting women. Considering he's drop-dead gorgeous and an all-around wonderful guy, it's hard to believe. But it's true."

"Isn't that funny? My neighbor, Greg, says the same thing," Cheryl added. She'd apparently decided her nail color was appropriate since she was now using a hand mirror to inspect her eyebrows. "He's not exactly look-ing for a permanent relationship, but he'd like to meet a woman who feels the same way about relationships. You know. Someone he can take to professional func-tions and all."

It wasn't long before all six women seated in the spa's

pool contributed names and statistics of a man who was perfect—just not perfect for them.

"Why didn't we ever talk about this before?" Rita said, as she stepped out of the pool and picked up one of the towels provided for the spa clients. She blotted the water from her skin. "Each of us knows at least one man who's dating material. What we should do is pool our resources and help each other out. I know I wouldn't mind meeting Josh Miller if he's that cute."

"Oh, he is."

Barbara also got out of the water, gathered up a towel, and reclined on one of the chaise longues stationed near the pool.

"You know what we need? We need a hotline for women who want a date," she quipped. "Or work up a monthly newsletter. How many other women are in the same position we are?"

"I would say more than you know," a lightly accented voice intruded.

The women looked up as a woman stepped outside the building, onto the concrete surrounding the heated pool. With her dark hair swept up in an elaborate twist and slim body dressed in cream-colored silk pants and matching blouse, she was the picture of European elegance. With her picture gracing the brochures that publicized the beauty salon and day spa, it was understandable why it was usually fully booked.

"Not you, CeCe," Barbara said. "I imagine men are lined up around the block just waiting to take you out."

"Every woman likes the idea of a man appreciating her," CeCe told them. "If I were you, I would see how many others know an eligible man the way you do. Professional women network all the time for business contacts. Why not for social contacts, also?''

"Blind Date Central." Rita laughed.

CeCe turned to her and smiled. "Exactly."

Chapter One

"I don't usually…" Gail waved her hand around in futile search for the words she required to get her point across.

"Go on blind dates." Brian provided them for her.

Her head bobbed. She looked down and found the napkin she held between her fingers turned to confetti. She flushed and quickly pushed the pieces to the side.

"It's just that they're so…" She waved one hand in the air as if again hoping she could pluck the errant word out of her surroundings.

"Scary?"

Her sudden laughter erupted into an unladylike snort. She quickly covered it up by grabbing her coffee cup and burying her nose in it.

"You sound as if you've done this before." Dr. Gail Roberts looked at him as if she couldn't believe the man seated across from her needed to lower himself to go on a blind date. Like she was.

Brian shrugged. "I've been on a few. All of them my sister, Nikki's idea. She thinks I don't get out enough, so she does her best to make sure I'm not sitting at home staring at the TV every night."

She refused to believe this man spent his free time

watching television. He didn't look the couch potato type.

He shrugged again. "My work keeps me busy, so I enjoy some vegetation time when I can get it."

Gail nodded. She knew his duties as a paramedic with the county fire department would keep him busy just as hers as a pediatrician did. So far she'd learned he was thirty-four, two years her senior, had become a paramedic because he knew he wasn't cut out to be a fireman, lived in a house he was planning to fix up and was the middle child of two brothers and two sisters. No bad habits, was polite and admitted he could cook without poisoning anyone.

He was all wrong for what she needed.

First of all, he was too tall. She preferred her men to be only a few inches above her five foot seven inches. He was a good six foot two. He was also not her type. In his jeans and navy blue T-shirt with a fire department crest adorning a pocket on his chest, he was casual to her dressy wardrobe. With his dark-brown hair and startling blue eyes, it was much too easy to be fascinated by this man. A man who was too, well, too…male.

She started to pick up her coffee cup again but stopped herself in time. No reason to drink coffee when the cup barely had a swallow left in it. She managed a weak smile when Brian recognized her predicament and signaled to the waitress for a refill.

She hated being here basically interviewing a man for a date! If she had her way, she wouldn't have even been here. But the medical association banquet was coming up in a little less than two weeks. Her physician's assistant, Sheila, flatly told her she shouldn't attend it alone. She should round up a date, pronto. Trouble was, Gail wasn't seeing anyone recently, and she couldn't think of anyone she'd care to ask to go with her. Sheila's teasing idea of using an escort service horrified Gail, and she stated she'd rather go alone. She should have made Sheila interview her date. The woman would have been in seventh heaven.

It wasn't until she went in for her twice-a-month manicure when her manicurist suggested she take a look at the spa's blind date central board that Gail found an answer to her dilemma.

An answer that now sat across from her.

She should have known that studying a picture on a board and sitting across from the real thing were entirely different. Pictures didn't have the vitality the real thing had. Pictures didn't smell like spice or look like every woman's fantasy. She wasn't ready for this!

Before now, she wouldn't have believed it was possible to choose a member of the opposite sex based purely on looks. She called women who did that shallow. So what does she do? She goes out and chooses a man because he has blue eyes. She was always a sucker for blue eyes. She also couldn't believe a man could look that good in jeans that were molded to a killer body and a T-shirt that caressed a chest Batman would have envied.

She wasn't against him because he had a blue-collar job. She was no snob, even if her parents had tried to raise her to be one. She refused to admit it was because there was something about him that struck a nerve deep inside her, and now that it had been struck she preferred to keep that nerve silent.

Even though time was running out on her, she could still smile, say how nice it was to meet him and as politely as possible tell him she was sorry to waste his time. She'd have to look elsewhere.

There was always Dr. Clooney, the dermatologist who'd broadly hinted they could attend the dinner together and maybe stop by his apartment for a nightcap later. There was only one problem with that scenario. George looked more like George of the Jungle than George Clooney, actor. If it came down to that, she'd be better off going alone.

"The dinner is formal, so I'll pay for the tuxedo rental," she informed him, surprised that the words coming out of her mouth weren't what she expected. *She was supposed to tell him he was off the hook! Wait a minute. Who says he'd say yes? Maybe he wouldn't consider her his type.*

"Don't worry about it. I never have a problem getting a tuxedo if I need one," Brian assured her. A small smile played about his lips.

Was he amused with her? What did she say that was so amusing? She wasn't sure she liked that.

"Yes, well." Gail pulled her business card case out of her purse and quickly wrote across the back of a white card. "My home number and pager number," she explained. "I don't like taking calls at my office unless they're emergencies. I'll have more details for you in a few days. The dinner is a week from Friday. Would that be a problem for you?"

Brian accepted the card and glanced at the neat script. "I thought all doctors wrote in strange hieroglyphics no mere mortal could comprehend."

"That's only when we write prescriptions," she said stiffly.

From the moment they shook hands when they first met, Brian was afraid that Gail didn't have one humorous bone in her body. From the moment she sat down and ordered her decaf cappuccino, Brian noticed she'd been as serious as if she were interviewing a prospective employee. Nothing in the past half hour had changed his mind about her.

Brian was used to women who laughed, who enjoyed life. He had a pretty good idea that Gail did little of either. No wonder she was looking for a date. He guessed her aloof "touch-me-not" manner would send most men running in the opposite direction. It should have put him off. It only took two seconds in her company to see she liked to keep herself distant. It wasn't long before he was ready to make an excuse and escape with both their dignities intact. Then she stumbled over her words in trying to explain why blind dates weren't her thing.

Maybe this wouldn't be so bad after all.

Brian snagged a napkin and quickly wrote on the white surface. "I'm off duty then, so no problem. Here's the firehouse number," he told her. "I'll be there for the next four days."

She carefully folded the napkin and tucked it into her purse. She glanced none too discreetly at her watch. She dredged up a cheery smile.

"Thank you for meeting with me, Brian," she almost stumbled over his name as if she realized what she'd intended to say wasn't what came out. "I really appreciate you helping me out with my dilemma."

"My mama taught me to never turn down a free meal." He grinned. He could tell by the slight tightening of her lips she didn't appreciate his type of humor.

"Yes, well, I have some appointments." She reached for her purse and opened it.

"I'll get this." He leaned forward in his chair and tucked his hand into his back pocket. He froze as his fingers only encountered a bit of lint. Not wanting to panic just yet, he surreptitiously checked his front pockets. Nothing. Heat stained his cheeks as he looked at Gail. "I guess I left my wallet at home. I was running late and showered and changed before coming over here. It's probably sitting on my chest of drawers."

"No problem. Besides, this should be my treat. I invited you." She offered him a cool smile and picked up the bill.

"I'll pay you back," Brian assured her as they later walked outside to the parking lot.

"No need to." She merely glanced at him as she headed for her red BMW convertible.

Ironically, Brian's pickup truck was parked in the next space.

Gail registered minor horror at the sight of a truck she was convinced should have been sent to the junkyard sometime after World War II.

"We'll take my car that evening," she stated, as she disarmed her alarm system and got in.

Brian watched her drive off.

"It's only one evening. The princess will have her Prince Charming and after that, we won't have to see each other again. Hopefully, they won't be serving chicken," he said, climbing into the truck.

"TELL ME ALL. Is he cute? What does he do? Does he have a brother?" Sheila Walters, Gail's physician's assistant, demanded to know as she walked into Gail's office.

Gail thought of his glossy dark-brown hair cut short, tanned skin, firm jaw, blue eyes that seemed to look into a person's soul and his smile that sent her stomach spinning. She feared she was taking on more than she could handle.

"Brian appears to be suitable even if he's not really my type. He's a paramedic with the fire department and seems nice. Actually, I'm sure the two of you would get along much better than he and I would. I'll give him your number after the banquet," she said offhandedly.

"Give him a chance first. Maybe the two of you will hit it off."

Gail studied the contents of the file. "I doubt it. I'm not the beer and barbecue type," she murmured.

"Oh come on, Gail, you couldn't be a snob if you tried," she chided. She perched herself on the edge of Gail's desk.

Gail looked around her office. As a pediatrician, she wanted her young patients to feel comfortable, not intimidated.

Dr. Seuss prints dominated the walls instead of diplomas, and a boldly colored plastic table and two chairs sat in one corner with a variety of toys strewn across it. Large plush animals that could be held and hugged by small hands sat in each chair awaiting their tiny admirers. All of the staff wore scrubs with cartoon characters scattered on the fabric, and even Gail's lab coats had cartoon characters embroidered on the pockets. All the examination rooms were likewise decorated to appeal to the young mind. She was convinced her small patients would relax when they entered her office, and she was right.

Pediatrician Gail Roberts, known for her no-nonsense manner toward her pint-size patients, looked more like one of her patients than an adult. She played with the stuffed bear perched on a corner of her desk.

"If I had my way I wouldn't even go to the banquet. It will be boring. The food is always terrible and the people pretentious," she muttered.

"Do not whine, Gail Ann Roberts. You have a date for the banquet, and you will go and have fun," Sheila said firmly, using the voice that worked well with her teenage sons.

Before Gail could stop her, Sheila picked up the picture and accompanying note that lay near the invitation.

"Never been married. Has no bad habits," Sheila read out loud. "Hmm, depends on what he considers bad habits. A real sweetheart. The man actually knows how to cook. Beware! He's hotter than a steam engine!" She raised an eyebrow. "My my." She held up the photograph that originally caught Gail's attention. It wasn't a beefcake type of photo like so many of the others. This man was wearing jeans and a white T-shirt with some sort of emblem on the chest pocket. Dark-brown hair cut short on top and along the sides. Her gaze took it all in. Firm jaw, strong cheekbones, winning smile displaying white teeth and a pair of dazzling blue eyes.

"No one has eyes that blue," Gail whispered, forgetting she wasn't alone. She didn't know why she took the photo and note down off the board. Or laid it here where she could see it. Where Sheila could see it and draw her own conclusions.

She stared at the engraved invitation that lay nearby. Anyone seeing the expression on her face would have assumed the invitation was to a disaster instead of a prestigious social affair.

She looked up with an engaging smile on her lips. "You love to party, Sheila. And this one will be filled with doctors from every speciality. A lot of them are single. You just might find Dr. Right. And while you're there, you could pick up my award for me."

The physician's assistant rolled her eyes. "Oh no,

you're not going to get out of it that easy. Come on, Gail. You'll have fun. You've already got the guy. Now you just need to find yourself a sexy dress and go and have yourself one wild time.''

Sheila took the bear out of Gail's hands. ''Now back to work for you. Adorable Adam is coming in for booster shots.''

Gail moaned and dropped her head onto her desktop. She covered her head with her hands and just sat there.

''No! Not today! Not Adam! He's my most ornery patient.''

''Stop whining,'' Sheila ordered, not showing one whit of sympathy. ''Something tells me Adam will be on his best behavior today.''

Gail shrugged on her lab coat. Daffy Duck, wearing a lab coat and stethoscope, was embroidered on the pocket. Her own stethoscope had a small fuzzy bear attached to the tubing.

''You just wait. The day will come when we'll see Adam on one of those tabloid shows,'' she said. ''He'll be the one the FBI is looking for.''

''No, he's too smart to settle for small time. He'll end up in politics,'' Sheila argued. ''He's got a winning smile that makes you believe he's innocent when we know different. Look on the bright side. After Adam, you can escape to the gym to work off your insanity and after that, relax with a facial and manicure.''

With that kind of incentive, Gail had no problem in picking up the pace.

''SO YOU'RE REALLY GOING to some fancy banquet with that doctor?'' Mark Walker asked his brother as he tossed a football across the yard.

"Mom always said not to refuse a free meal." He threw it back.

"So, what's she like?"

"Okay-looking if you like the uptight type. She's a doctor and came across kinda stuck-up. I guess knowing I have a blue-collar job and actually seeing me was two different things. She's got the ultimate topless yuppie-mobile that she insisted we'll be taking to the banquet. Guess she didn't like my wheels." He grinned. "I had Dad's truck that day."

"Maybe it wasn't so much the truck putting her off as her meeting the wrong brother," Mark joked. "Maybe she needs to meet your handsome brother."

"Maybe she does. If I had one." He expelled a burst of air when the football landed against his midsection.

Mark didn't look the least bit sorry for what he did. "Did Dad tell you when your car will be ready?"

"His usual answer. 'It's ready when I say so.'" Brian tossed the ball from one hand to the other. "You know Dad. You push him and you'll never see your vehicle again." He threw the ball back.

Since their father was known to be the best mechanic in the county, Mark heartily agreed.

"Tell you what, little brother. I'd be more than willing to take your place with the lady. I always did like women driving topless." He tossed the ball up and down before throwing it back to Brian. "Maybe she'll be willing to give me a physical."

"Oh yeah, and once she's done she'll give you a lollipop. She's a pediatrician, dork." Brian deliberately threw it hard and fast toward his brother's midriff. Mark's mouth opened, emitting a painful *"Woof!"*

when it connected. "Come to think of it, you would qualify."

Mark held the football over his head as he tried to catch his breath. "Not nice," he wheezed.

Brian snickered. "Yeah, I know."

"For that, you have to spring for the beer."

"After seeing you at a loss for words, for once I'm willing to pay."

Mark tossed the football toward the back steps and headed for his brother. He draped an arm around Brian's shoulders.

"Good, 'cuz I'm really thirsty. And while I'm enjoying my beer you can tell me all about your future with the cute doctor."

"There is no future," Brian insisted. "I'm doing her a favor by taking her to some fancy banquet and then we go our own ways. Right after I kill Nikki for getting me into this."

"After you're sent to prison for the rest of your life, can I have your car?"

"Nah, I thought I'd give it to Dad, but I bet if you ask real nice he'll give you his truck."

"Are you kidding? Dad's talking about being buried in that truck."

"YOU'RE NOT a real doctor." The boy stood with legs splayed apart, his arms crossed in front of him. The look he gave Gail was filled with suspicion.

"What makes you think I'm not a real doctor?" she asked, seating herself on a bright-red leather stool so she would be at his eye level.

He sneered as he looked around the room. "There's no pictures of naked ladies showing where all the insides are. And I don't see a skeleton." He stared at her through narrowed eyes. "You just don't look like a real doctor."

"Would you like to see my diplomas from medical school?" she asked, used to this form of questioning.

"You get a good enough printer you can make 'em up." He sat down, his legs swinging.

Gail read the file of her newest patient. She silently condemned her receptionist to a dire fate for giving her this obstacle at the end of the day when she needed to get to Steppin' Out to get her hair and nails done and get home to dress.

A vision of the dress drifted across her mind. She'd paid more for it than she'd planned to pay for a dress, but it called to her. She usually wore dinner suits to these affairs, but this time she decided to try something different. This dress was about as different as you could get. That she bought the dress with Brian Walker in mind was something she chose not to think about.

For now, all she had to do is convince Thad Rogers she was most definitely a doctor and qualified to give him his booster shots. Then she'd be out of there. Thad finally agreed, but it wasn't easy.

Gail didn't have time to think from when she left her office to when she arrived at the salon and later at her town house.

"It's only for one night. Better I take a date than attend alone," she muttered, washing her face and pulling out her makeup. The image of the ancient pickup truck drifted through her mind. Her hand wobbled as she applied champagne-colored eye shadow. "Just because we have nothing in common doesn't mean we can't enjoy the evening." She moaned as she realized she was lying to herself. "This will teach me to choose a man for his blue eyes."

NOT ONE WORD came to mind. For a man who always had the right thing to say at the right time, he was finally at a loss for words.

"Honestly, you look as if you've never seen a woman before," Gail grumbled, stepping past him so she could enter his house. "What have you done with your tie?"

He tried to clear his throat. "Tried to tie it," he croaked, hanging on to the ends.

Gail shook her head. "I don't think so." She brushed his hands away and swiftly tied a perfect bow.

Brian couldn't breathe. Where was the efficient-looking woman he met last week? He knew she wouldn't be wearing the sensible pants and high-necked blouse she wore when they first met. At the same time, he didn't expect she'd wear a red dress guaranteed to stop traffic.

The artfully cut bodice and thin straps left little to the imagination while the semi-sheer skirt flared around her calves. Even her high heels were nothing more than narrow straps of leather crisscrossing her feet. Her makeup made her brown eyes look as if they had gold flecks in them. Her lips, with a shimmery red gloss highlighting them, looked kissable.

No doctor should smell this good, he told himself, as he stood still while she dispensed with the tie.

"You look very nice," she said crisply, stepping back and examining her work. "Are you ready?"

"And willing," he quipped with a grin.

She didn't grin in return.

"I've heard smiling doesn't smudge lipstick," he said dryly, following her outside.

Two chirps sounded as she disarmed the car alarm. He barely touched his fingers to the door handle when she stopped him.

"I don't allow smoking in my car," she warned him.

"No problem. The only smoking in my house is when I burn something when I'm cooking." Brian folded his six-foot-plus frame into the passenger seat of the BMW. He eyed the gleaming red hood. "Just off the showroom floor?"

"It's relatively new."

Brian nodded. "Then I guess you still park it out in the boonies and want to see a parking valet's driving record before he's allowed to get behind the wheel. If you don't mind a suggestion, the freeway is backed up at this hour. It will be much quicker reaching the hotel via surface streets."

"All right." She bypassed the freeway on-ramp. Even from below they could see the line of cars that weren't going anywhere fast.

She sped up as she reached an intersection, sailing blithely through a yellow light.

"As for parking valets, I only want to make sure they haven't been convicted of grand theft auto," she informed him.

He flashed her a second look filled with surprise. *No, it had to be his imagination. There was no way this lady could have a sense of humor.*

A frown furrowed her brow as she quickly examined something on the dashboard.

"And here I was told they did such a great job at detailing," she muttered. 'Look at that smudge.''

Scratch the idea she has a sense of humor.

Brian stuck his finger in his shirt collar in hopes of loosening it a bit. He was certain he'd be strangled by the end of the evening.

"Again I do thank you for accompanying me this evening," Gail said stiffly. She slowed the moment she saw the traffic light turn yellow.

"No problem. I never mind pulling out the old tux for an evening of fun," he said glibly.

Whatever Gail was going to say when she turned to face him was halted as an indistinct figure seemed to flow next to the driver's door. Light gleamed against the metal pressed against her temple.

"Nice car, sweetheart. You don't mind giving it up, do you?"

She stared wide-eyed at Brian even as the heavy body odor filled the car.

Brian kept his hands placed lightly on his thighs. He didn't want to spook the guy into doing something stupid.

"Give it up?" she squeaked.

"Yeah. It's so nice I think we'll take it." The man opened the rear door and slid inside while still keeping his gun aimed at Gail's head. Another man slid in behind Brian. Cold metal jabbed the back of his head.

"Just take my wallet and go," Gail insisted in a shaky voice keeping a tight grip on the steering wheel.

"Oh, we'll take your wallet, baby. And your boyfriend's. But we want the car, too. Go." Her head snapped forward as he jabbed the gun barrel in the back of her head. "And don't go so fast you attract a cop's attention, or you'll find your blood splattered all over the pretty upholstery."

"Considering she just had it detailed, I don't think she'd want the mess," Brian said mildly. He winced when his abductor slapped the gun barrel against the back of his head.

"Don't be a smart-ass," the man snarled.

Brian bit back the reply he wanted to make. There was no mistaking the fear etched on Gail's face. He already knew with a gun jammed against his head it wouldn't be a good idea to try to be a hero and do something that would end up stupid. Or deadly.

The silence in the car was charged with fear and tension as the man behind Gail gave her terse orders as to when and where to turn. It wasn't long before the city lights grew fewer and farther between. As did traffic. In the dim light from the dashboard, Brian could see her swallowing hard when she was directed to park on a side road.

He gauged the odds against them and knew they were high. Was there a chance he could somehow jump both guys and give her a chance to make a run for it? Would she do it if she could?

"Get out!" the lead man shouted, waving the gun.

Gail stumbled as she climbed out of the car. She grasped the side of the car to keep her balance.

"Look—" she began.

"Shut up!"

She froze.

Brian growled a curse and stepped forward when the man's hand lashed out toward Gail. She cried out when he pulled her necklace from her neck. Brian's fist was cocked back, ready to land a punch when the pain exploded in the back of his head. He suddenly couldn't stand up straight and felt himself folding downward like a puppet whose strings had been cut.

"Brian!" Gail's scream sounded as if it was traveling through a tunnel.

He was past caring because the darkness surrounding him was much too comforting. His last thought seemed to echo inside his head.

The tux shop sure won't be happy to have bullet holes in its suit.

Chapter Two

"Brian? Brian! Brian, you have to wake up! Please, wake up!"

He wondered if this was what being dead felt like. Except that voice kept intruding.

Oh damn, he must be in hell if Dr. Straight and Narrow was here.

He slitted his eyes but could see nothing. He opened them wider and started to lift his head. He hissed when what seemed like a major fireworks display from the Fourth of July went off inside his head.

"Be careful, you might have a concussion," Gail warned, refusing to allow him to sit up.

He took a deep breath, which hurt like crazy. His head felt as if it was in pieces, obviously been punched or kicked in the side, and he was positive some bug was traveling up his right thigh. Aches and pains. Nothing to indicate any bullet holes.

But he was still alive.

"How long have I been out?" he croaked, closing his eyes against the pain. What he wouldn't give for a couple heavy duty aspirin!

"At least a couple minutes. They haven't been gone

very long. They took my watch, so I couldn't time it," she replied, her tone crisp.

He raised his head a bit, didn't feel any nausea or notice any double vision. He tried a little bit more until he was sitting up.

"No concussion," he concluded.

"How would you know?" she argued.

Brian sighed. The last thing he needed right now was an argument. "I'm a paramedic, remember? I probably see more concussions than you do."

"And I'm a doctor and more qualified to diagnose one."

"Yeah, well, a few extra years in school doesn't mean you know about concussions unless you've had one. I've had a few so I know what one feels like." He squinted to see the dark shadow he guessed to be Gail. "Are you okay?"

"Other than having my car stolen, my purse taken, my jewelry snatched off my body, and being left out in the middle of nowhere, I'm just fine," she snapped.

Brian reached inside his jacket.

"They took your wallet and watch, too."

He took his time getting to his feet. He wasn't about to disgrace himself by falling on his face after finding out he hadn't been killed after all. For a moment, the world around him swam, but by sheer will he felt his senses returning to normal. He slowly turned in a tight circle hoping to see a familiar landmark. So far, not one tree looked familiar.

"Any idea where we are?"

Her sigh was resigned. "No."

Okay, good, she's not having hysterics.

He doubted his aching head could take any screaming. He gingerly touched the back of his head and winced

when a shot of pain warned him he found what he was
looking for. When his fingers came away wet he knew
he found what he'd suspected he would. Good thing it
was dark. He always hated the sight of his own blood.

"They've just left us out in the middle of nowhere,"
Gail ranted, waving her arms around. "What are we
supposed to do out here? They took my purse, which
has my cell phone, my car, which I haven't even made
the first payment for," her voice began to rise.

"Oh, hell," he muttered. "Why don't you be grateful
for small miracles. Such as the fact they didn't kill us
and dump our bodies in a ditch."

"They may as well have done just that! We haven't
seen one car in either direction for the last half hour,"
she argued. "There's no sign of life anywhere around
here."

Brian pulled in a deep breath. "You know, things
would have been a hell of a lot easier if the carjackers
had just kept you. But I guess they decided I needed to
be punished for some misdeed in my past." He waved
off her squawking protest. "I apologize. Consider it insanity for what we're going through. What we need to
do now is find a phone."

Gail crossed her arms in front of her chest. "And, of
course, you'll find a call box right around the corner.
Except there isn't any corner to go around!"

He pressed his hands against his forehead. "Damn,
you're worse than a fire siren. Look at it this way. We
have no choice. I don't see any lights in the distance,
so there aren't any houses nearby. We're clearly on a
side road that has to lead to somewhere."

"Or not," she spat out.

He sighed. "Or not. If we're going to find someone
to help us, we'll have to walk."

"Walk!" Gail protested with the fury of a woman who was clearly out of her element. "I paid two hundred dollars for these shoes! They're not made for walking!"

"Two hundred dollars?" he roared back then regretted it instantly when pain zigzagged a path through his head. "You know what, I don't care if they cost you two thousand dollars and you can only walk on silk carpets with them. We're walking out of here in the direction we came. Don't even think for a moment that I'll carry you." Now that his eyes had accustomed themselves to the dark he could see the expression on her face. It didn't bode well.

"All right, Mister Macho can find his way without a map. Which way did we come in?"

Brian looked one way then the other. He couldn't find anything in either direction to tell the difference. He was feeling well on his way past disgust. If the guys found out about this catastrophe, they'd never let him live it down.

"Oh, hell." He closed his eyes, fervently praying when he opened them again she would be gone, and he'd be in bed. He opened them. No such luck.

He looked both ways again.

"We go this way."

"How do you know that's the way to go?" Suspicion laid heavily on her words.

"I just do." There was no way he'd admit he chose blindly. Something told him she'd never let it rest.

Ignoring his aching head, he put one foot in front of the other and started walking down the road. He didn't bother looking to see if Gail was following him. Maybe it wasn't the gentlemanly thing to do, but right now he was past caring. All he wanted was to find a phone and get someone out here to take them back into the city.

"I can't walk among all these rocks in these shoes!" Gail wailed, stumbling after him.

"Then take them off."

"Very funny." She wrapped her arms around herself as her gaze darted about. "Do you think there's any wild animals out here?"

"Oh, I couldn't be that lucky."

She narrowed her eyes at his back. If only there had been a target painted there. "What did you say?"

"Maybe a few duckies," he said in a louder, clearer voice.

"Yeah, right," she muttered, her arms windmilling to keep her balance when she stumbled on a rock. "Most men carry a cell phone on their belt loop or something." She wanted to blame someone, and right now, he was her best option. "'Take surface streets,'" you said. "'You'll get there faster,'" you said. Get faster where? *The entrance to hell?*"

Brian halted and turned around.

"So you're saying it's my fault?"

"If the shoe fits." She sneered. "We might have been doing the stop-and-go tango on the freeway, but I wouldn't have lost my car to two carjackers!"

He walked back to her and aggressively thrust his face in hers. "Don't worry, sweetheart, maybe they'll only take it for a joyride and not take it to some chop shop."

Her eyes dilated, and the breath left her lungs in a rush. "Chop shop?" She didn't want to think about what it meant.

"Yeah, chop shop. You know, car thieves taking their loot to an out-of-the-way garage and taking the car apart piece by piece until there's nothing left but a hollow shell," he enunciated each word. "And then they sell those parts for other cars."

For a moment, Gail felt as if she were having a heart attack. "You take that back."

"It is not my fault we were carjacked," Brian informed her in a cold voice. "It just happened because you had a hot little car two thugs wanted. Nothing more. It could have happened to you on the way to or from work. It could have happened to you when you parked at the grocery store. Think about that. And think that if it had been someone else, you might not have been dumped somewhere in one piece. Instead, you might have been cut up into little pieces and dumped in a ditch somewhere. A lot worse things could have happened. Just be grateful you're still alive."

"I didn't want to go to this lousy banquet, but my physician's assistant said it would be good for me!" she wailed.

Brian shook his head and turned around, heading off again. Gail had no choice but to follow.

With each step, she muttered a new curse.

"Do me a favor and button the lip," he ordered.

She glared at his back. "Excuse me?"

Brian stopped so quickly Gail bumped into his back.

"In other words, zip the lip, put a sock in it, wear a muzzle, stifle yourself, hush the mouth, cease and desist, silence is golden. In other words, *shut up!*"

She opened her mouth prepared to argue back then snapped it shut. Except she couldn't let it go.

"I could have chosen a renowned dermatologist to take me to this dinner."

He swung around and started walking again. "Maybe you should have. He might have been able to help you out with that little blemish you have under your chin."

Gail gasped and instinctively reached for her purse.

Except it wasn't there. She silently cursed Brian into oblivion and began walking.

Her calves burned, her thighs screamed, her toes hurt, her soles ached, and her heels felt as if they were punched with sharp nails. She vowed from now on she'd visit the fitness center more often. Obviously going three times a week wasn't good enough to keep her in shape for the kind of hike Brian was taking her on.

At the moment, she would have killed for a flashlight.

Better yet, to wake up in her bed and find out this was nothing more than a bad dream.

"All right, fine, things could be worse," she muttered.

"You just had to say it, didn't you?" Brian shouted above the roar of rain falling on them. "It's not enough we're making our way down a dark road without a person or even a house in sight, no, you had to say things could be worse!"

"Right, I called up the local rainmaker and asked for a downpour!" Gail was angry enough to cry, but with her face already wet from the rain she couldn't tell if there were tears there, too.

They were doomed. She was positive of it. No sooner had she uttered the words that things couldn't get worse, when the heavens opened up and dumped the Pacific Ocean on their heads.

Gail thought of her new dress that now uncomfortably stuck to her body and shoes that felt as if they were falling apart from all the mud and water. Both were ruined. Just as ruined as her beloved car that was probably in a thousand pieces by now.

And the banquet where her name would be called and she wouldn't be there to accept her award. Her stomach even had the audacity to remind her it hadn't been fed since breakfast.

Instead of eating a meal and pretending she was enjoying herself, she was walking through rain and mud on a deserted road with a man she didn't know.

She was positive blisters were forming upon blisters by the time Brian grabbed her arm.

"Look over there," he said pointing away from the road.

She squinted but could only see indistinct shapes. "At what?"

"A mailbox." Triumph deepened his voice. "And where there's a mailbox, there's..."

"People!" She started to jump up and down but slipped in the mud instead. If Brian hadn't been holding on to her arm, she would have easily fallen on her face. She quickened her pace as he led her down what should have been a driveway instead of a sea of mud and holes. "Hasn't anyone heard about paving driveways out here?"

"Maybe this is a back road to the house," Brian replied.

Gail's hopes started to fall when they reached the small house with its darkened windows.

"Maybe they go to bed early?" she said hopefully, already thinking of a hot shower, hot coffee and dry clothes.

Brian made a tour of the exterior. "No, it looks as if it's deserted." He led her around to the rear of the house. "Maybe it's someone's vacation house. It looks too well maintained to be abandoned." He looked around then picked up a rock.

"What are you doing?"

"Getting us inside and out of the rain." He carefully

broke the window set in the back door then reached through. Within a minute, he had ushered Gail inside.

"What if they have an alarm system?" she protested.

"Then we won't have to worry about a thing because the cops will show up, and we can explain we're not burglars. Just carjack victims. Don't worry, I'll leave a note promising to pay for the window."

While she was now out of the rain, she could feel the cold even more. She shivered, hugging herself in an attempt to get warm. Brian tried the light switch but nothing happened.

"No electricity, I'm afraid." He reached for the phone on the wall and picked it up. "Phone's disconnected."

She watched him move around the room opening and closing drawers and cabinet doors. On the heels of Brian's soft exclamation of triumph a beam of light flashed in her direction.

"At least the batteries in the flashlight are still good," he said, sweeping the light over the kitchen. He took her hand and led her through the house until they found the family room.

Gail cast a longing glance at the fireplace.

"Please tell me you were a Boy Scout," she pleaded.

"There's got to be matches around here. Don't worry, I'll get a fire going," he promised. "I saw a filled wood box out by the back door and luckily, it remained dry. Why don't you take the flashlight and find us some towels so we can dry off?"

She took it and shone the light ahead of her as she wandered down a hallway, looking through doorways until she found what turned out to be a linen closet. The towels smelled a little musty but she didn't care. She wrapped her hair in one and threw another around her shoulders while she pulled out a few more for Brian. When she returned to the family room she found him squatting in front of the fireplace. The crackling fire sent out a welcome warmth to the cold and wet intruders.

"These should help," she said, dropping the towels near him.

He looked up and grinned. "Thanks."

"I'll check the kitchen. Maybe the stove is gas and if it's still turned on, I could make us some coffee," she offered, feeling that nerve struck again. She couldn't believe his smile could generate that kind of feeling after the kind of night she'd just had.

"Good idea. Maybe even some food." He started rubbing his head with a towel.

It didn't take Gail long to discover the stove was electric, and there was nothing they could use to make coffee over the fire. She wished she could find some chocolate powder and powdered milk. She would have enjoyed trying to make hot chocolate over the fire. What she did find, she loaded on a tray and carried into the room. By then, the fire had been going long enough to comfortably warm the room.

"Found these while I did some looking around," Brian announced, piling blankets and a couple of sweatshirts on the couch. "You'd be better off getting out of those wet clothes before you catch pneumonia."

She cocked an eyebrow. "Trying to practice medicine without a license again?"

"Just remembering something my mom taught us." He stood up and shrugged off his dinner jacket. He loosened his tie and pulled it free. His once snowy white shirt, now a vague muddy color, was next to go.

Gail's mouth turned dry as the firelight allowed her to see an incredible male torso before it was covered with dark fleece. His wasn't the first man's bare chest she'd seen. It was just the best she'd seen.

"Yes, good idea," she croaked then coughed to cover her confusion. "No luck finding anything we could cook, but I did find a bottle of wine, some crackers that aren't entirely stale, Cheez Whiz and two cans of salted peanuts." She held up her tray.

"Right now, it sounds gourmet to me." He laid out the blankets on the floor and sat down, gesturing for her to sit also.

Gail pulled the sweatshirt over her head, almost moaning her joy in the sensation of dry warm fabric surrounding her. She was delighted to see that it fell down to her knees. She kicked off her shoes and sat down next to Brian. He topped a cracker with cheese and handed it to her. She bit down and agreed with Brian.

"Better than caviar," she declared.

"Considering I hate caviar, that could say a lot," Brian joked, pouring wine into the two glasses Gail also brought.

"I'm not too fond of it myself," she admitted, fixing a cracker for Brian and handing it to him.

He stretched out on his side, his upper body braced on one arm. One hand circled the wineglass stem.

"And here I thought you'd be eating caviar every night of the week."

Gail sipped the wine. She waved her hand to indicate it would take her a moment to answer.

"I guess it's an acquired taste like eating oysters or avocados," she said. She suddenly realized she was feeling more relaxed than she had in some time. Funny she would feel that way with Brian after all that had happened. "Ten to one there would have been caviar and oysters at the banquet. I'm not that fond of oysters, either.'' She made a face.

''If you didn't want to go, why were you going?''

She pushed up the sleeves of the sweatshirt and leaned back using the couch as a backboard. She was reluctant to say why even though he would have found out if they'd made it to the banquet.

''I was supposed to receive an award.'' She tried to pass it off as something unimportant even though she'd been thrilled when she first heard the news.

''Really?'' His interest was patently sincere. ''For what?''

Gail looked away. It was easier to look at the fire than at Brian's face. Most of the men she'd dated in the past hadn't been interested in what had become so important to her.

''About eighteen months ago, I started a support group among some of my patients,'' she said slowly. ''With more teen pregnancies happening, I was suddenly finding myself with pregnant preteens. While I always referred them to an obstetrician, some of them still called me because they felt more comfortable with me. Once a week we meet, and I try to bring in speakers that will help them with what they're going through physically and mentally. A few of them who have kept their babies are now bringing their babies in to me. I don't know why I'm getting the award since this has been done before.''

Brian shook his head. ''I've got to admire you. Babies having babies has to be rough. But if you're working with the kids, you're taking an extra step that maybe other pediatricians wouldn't take.''

''I just try to look at their needs and fill them,'' she explained, starting to gear up. ''Just as I realized some of my overweight patients needed help. Nutritional programs were all right, but they needed to voice their thoughts and anxieties without fear of ridicule. And when I could, I tried to get the family involved, too.''

He let loose a low whistle. ''You really go above and beyond for your patients, Doc.''

Gail tried to read his tone. She'd heard that phrase before and mockery was usually included. It didn't seem to be this time. She wasn't sure if it was the couple sips of wine she'd taken that had given her a warm feeling inside or Brian's words of praise.

''I just want to give them the best care I can,'' she said honestly.

''And it seems you do.'' His eyes softened. ''I'm sorry you won't get to accept your award, Gail. It sounds as if you truly deserve it. Something to put on your wall.''

She laughed. ''I don't think a plaque would go with my Dr. Seuss prints. Most of my patients wouldn't be impressed with an award the way they would with Horton on the wall.''

''What about the parents?''

She shrugged. ''They know I'm more concerned about the kids than showing off my diplomas.'' She nibbled daintily on another cracker. Her hungry stomach was thanking her for the sustenance. She took her blanket and wrapped it around her legs. ''You're acting awfully upbeat considering the position we're in.''

''What good would it do to moan and groan?'' he asked with a logic she had to admire. ''I'm looking at the bright side. We're out of the rain, we're warm and dry, and we have this excellent cuisine to dine on. You can't tell me that your dinner would have food this good.''

An unladylike snort erupted from Gail before she could stop it. She sipped her wine. "A green salad to start, then chicken with wine sauce, wild rice, baby carrots, and berry parfait for dessert. The committee for these dinners believes in the best."

Brian groaned loudly and fell back. "Damn! Baby carrots? I love baby carrots! Teenage carrots don't have near enough good taste the way baby carrots do." He sat up and grabbed a handful of peanuts and tossed one into the air and caught it in his open mouth. A second peanut quickly followed.

"Is this something they teach paramedics?" she asked, watching a third go the same route.

"Not just anyone can do this," he informed her with grave importance. "It takes years of practice and an agility most people can't even comprehend."

"Hmm." Gail leaned forward and scooped peanuts out of the can. She tipped her head back and opened her mouth. She flipped a peanut into the air and caught it with her mouth. After doing it several times, she tossed a smirk at Brian. "Doctors are well-known for their hand-eye coordination."

"Yeah, but can you do this?" Brian tilted his head back and carefully balanced a peanut on his nose. While his hands made drumming motions he snapped his face upward and caught the peanut in his mouth. He threw his arms out in a *ta-da!* gesture.

She didn't look impressed. "My neighbor's dog can do that with a Milk-Bone."

He wasn't the least bit fazed. "Yeah, but a peanut is a lot smaller than a Milk-Bone, therefore, harder to do. You should see me juggle oranges."

"You don't juggle hypodermics in front of patients, do you?"

"Only the ones who'd appreciate it." The firelight cast shadows across his face as he studied her. "Okay, where is she?"

Not a question she expected. "Where is who?"

"The uptight doc I met that first time."

Gail made a face as she remembered her thoughts that evening. "Interviewing blind dates isn't something I do on a regular basis." She covered a cracker with cheese and nibbled around the edges as was her habit. "Nor is getting carjacked an everyday event." She moaned softly as thoughts of what was probably happening to her beautiful new car came to mind.

"Hey." Brian swiftly moved forward and covered her hand with his. "Just remember that you can replace a car easier than you can replace yourself."

"Yes, but you ended up with a concussion," she reminded him.

"I do not have a concussion. Just a nasty bump on the head."

"Bumps on the head don't come as a result of a gun hitting you."

He shrugged. "Better a bump than a bullet."

Gail's face lost all trace of color as the realization of what could have happened hit her with the force of a tornado. She turned her hand until their palms touched. She curled her fingers around his and held on tight. The strangled sounds deep in her throat weren't pleasant. She stared at Brian, but his face took on a hazy quality as her world started to swim around her.

"Oh no, you don't." He palmed the back of her head and pressed it downward until her face met her knees. "Come on, sweetheart, just breathe slow and easy."

She wanted to tell him she couldn't breathe slow and easy, but all that came out were little hiccups. She waved her hands to tell him she was all right, but he clearly wasn't having any of it.

"Give it another minute," he ordered.

When he was finally satisfied she wouldn't pass out, he released her. Gail lifted her head and focused on Brian's intent features. She pushed his hands away and stood up. She opened her mouth to say something but nothing came out. In the end, she gave up and just bolted for the bathroom.

Brian winced when he heard sounds of retching from the bathroom. His first instinct was to go in and comfort her, but he doubted she'd appreciate his seeing her in such a vulnerable position.

He was deciding that maybe she wasn't so bad after all. After her snit about walking so far, she eventually came around. Even now, they weren't in the best position, but she seemed to be adapting. Except for the throwing up part.

When she returned, she looked vaguely embarrassed. She didn't meet his eyes as she seated herself on the couch, curling her feet under her.

Brian rose to his feet and went into the kitchen. A moment later, he returned with a glass of water. She accepted it with a smile of thanks and thirstily gulped the liquid.

"Sensory overload," he murmured, sitting down beside her. "Everyone goes through it."

A roll of thunder faintly sounded in the distance.

Gail collapsed against the back of the couch. "Don't tell me. You were just going to say at least we're not outside under a tree."

"There you go. Things are looking up already."

Brian's grin widened as Gail's expression grew longer. He was relieved color had returned to her face.

He guessed she'd washed her face while she was in there since the raccoon eyes her mascara had left under her eyes were now gone. He could see that even with a clean face, she was still less than immaculate. Their hike had left her dress tattered and shredded around the hemline. Her elegant upsweep hung limply down around her face. As if guessing the direction of his thoughts, she lifted her arms and pulled out hairpins, dropping them into her lap. She winced as she tried to finger-comb the knots from her hair.

"Come here." He grasped her hand and pulled her down onto the floor in front of him. He set her in between his legs with her back to him.

"What are you doing?" She tried to turn her head, but he pressed his hands on her shoulders.

"Don't worry. I have sisters, and I know what I'm doing. Man, what did your hairdresser use on your hair? Cement?" He pulled a comb out of his pants pocket. He carefully smoothed out a strand of hair then worked on the next strand. "I guess the rain stuck it all together."

Gail sat stiffly, waiting for pain from pulled hair. After it didn't happen, the feel of his hands on her hair started to soothe her. She closed her eyes and started to relax. She always enjoyed having her hair done because the shampoo girl always gave her a hair massage that left her tingling from head to toe. She never thought a rough-and-ready paramedic could do the same. Except this one did even better. She wasn't aware a soft sigh escaped her lips as her head started to tip forward. His hands left her hair and trailed their way down to her shoulders. Each knot in her upper back seemed to evaporate under his talented touch.

She smiled and tipped her head back further. "Don't

stop.'' Her words ended in a soft moan. She opened her eyes, meeting his.

Her moan suddenly froze in her throat as she met the seductive blue flame in his eyes. Just as suddenly, his hands slowed their movements. Caressing instead of massaging.

Brian tilted his head slightly and leaned forward. His mouth was a breath away from Gail's. Her lips parted in anticipation of what was to come. Their respiration slowed and each started to move just a bit closer to each other to finish what he started.

At that same moment, an earsplitting clap of thunder rocked the house on its foundation with the strength of an earthquake.

Chapter Three

The thunder broke them apart. They looked up simultaneously as if there would be more. For a moment, the panicked look on each face rivaled that of hormone-laden teenagers caught by a parent.

"Think someone's trying to tell us something?" Brian said hoarsely.

Gail scooted away from him and practically plastered herself against the couch. She presented a smile that was so bright it rivaled the lightning outside.

"More wine?" She held up the bottle.

He shook his head and held up his half-empty glass.

Brian couldn't miss the trapped animal look in Gail's eyes. He silently cursed Mother Nature for sending a loud and rude interruption at such an inopportune time.

He wasn't sure when the idea of kissing her came to mind. The thought blossomed when he saw the enticing shape of her lips. Then he knew he was going to kiss her. Instead of still enjoying that kiss, his ears rang from the thunderclap. He winced when a second one seemed to follow on the heels of the first.

"Looks like we're in for a major storm tonight," he muttered. "Good thing we found this place."

Gail nibbled on another cracker. "Let's just hope

lightning doesn't strike the house and set it on fire. The way our luck has been going, it could happen.''

"I thought you were finally looking on the bright side," he chided.

She proceeded to tick her grievances off on her fingertips. "Where shall I start? My brand-new car was stolen, my brand-new dress is ruined as are my brand-new shoes." She mournfully gazed at the delicate straps that made up her shoes. One heel hung loosely from the sole. They were only fit for the trash bin. "My manicure and pedicure are ruined. We won't even mention what happened to my hair and makeup. I'm stuck in a house that has no electricity, most of its food in cans and no manual can opener. I'm wearing a sweatshirt that smells like mothballs and drinking wine and eating whipped cheese on stale crackers with a man who's wearing a rented tuxedo that I can bet the tux shop won't take back." Her brow furrowed in thought. "Did they suggest you take out insurance?"

"Insurance?"

"You know, the way car rental companies offer insurance," she explained.

Brian nodded sagely. "Maybe I'll suggest that. Might be good for weddings that go bad. Prom dates that end up in a disaster."

"Maître d' who's come up against a bowl of bouillabaisse," Gail suggested, entering into the spirit of the game. "Symphony musician with a leaky instrument."

Brian, who'd been tossing peanuts into his mouth suddenly started choking so hard Gail slid off the couch and knelt beside him, thumping him on the back. When he recovered his breath, she handed him her glass of water.

"Thanks," he wheezed.

"At least I didn't have to perform a tracheotomy." She took the glass from him and set it to one side.

"Good thing, since I didn't have my penknife with me." As the words sunk in Brian took another look at Gail. She was definitely looking more relaxed. And if he wasn't mistaken, he'd swear there was a hint of amusement in the tilt of her lips.

He stared at her, narrowing his eyes in thought. Maybe there was hope for her after all.

Brian sat up straighter. "You're on a deserted island and can only take three books with you. What would they be and why?"

Gail turned her head so she could stare into the flames.

"*Emma* because the woman who thought she was the teacher was the one who learned. Any Clive Barker novel because I'd want something scary to read, and he's about as scary as you can get. *Gray's Anatomy* so I wouldn't forget the basics." She presented him with a cool smile. "Your turn."

He gave a quick shake of the head. "*Catch 22* because it was one of the first "adult" books I ever read. *The Hunt for Red October* because I like submarines. And *Centennial* because I enjoy reading history, and Michener did it so well." He leaned over and tossed a few sticks on the fire. Sparks flew up and landed harmlessly.

Gail tucked her legs under her and settled back against the couch.

"You're ten years old. You can go fishing with your best friend, go to the movies with your second best friend, or attend a birthday party where you can have all the cake and ice cream you can eat. The catch is, it's a boy-girl party, and you'll be expected to dance with a girl. Which will you choose?'' she asked.

"Go fishing with my best friend, persuade him to go to the movies with my second best friend, then persuade both of them to go with me to the party. If they're really my friends, they won't let me suffer alone,'' he said promptly.

"Not fair,'' she protested. "You're only supposed to choose one!''

"I'm a guy, sweetheart,'' he drawled. "And a guy who's ten years old will do all he can because he's afraid of missing out on something.''

Gail shook her head and covered her face with her hands. "That's not the way you play the game and you know it.'' Her words were muffled by her hands. "And don't call me sweetheart.''

"Can't help it. It's a guy thing.'' Brian eyed the can of peanuts but remembering what happened earlier decided to bypass them. "So, what about you? You're in high school and have the choice of—'' he paused for several moments, "dating the captain of the football team, becoming head cheerleader, or leading the debate club in the finals. Which is it?''

"The captain of the football team was conceited. I wasn't coordinated enough to even make cheerleader, but my debate skills were, and are, excellent. That's what looks good when one applies to universities.''

"You are good,'' Brian said with undisguised admiration.

"You're just as sneaky in figuring out what's your best option,'' she pointed out.

"Paramedics, like doctors, have to react fast. We're expected to think on our feet.''

"Why did you become a paramedic?" she asked, finding herself more curious about him.

Brian shrugged. "Nothing exciting about it. I was a medic in the army and when I got out, I found a way to use my skills."

"You could have gone to medical school."

He stretched out in front of the fireplace, his body propped up on one elbow. His sweatshirt tightened across his chest in a manner that had Gail remembering what was beneath it. Her fingers itched to discover what it felt like.

"No, thanks. I wasn't all that fond of school to begin with. Besides, I like working with the fire department. I like the variety and challenges I come up against. I might deliver a baby one day and help a man having a heart attack the next," he explained. "I've made good friends within the department and have made a nice life for myself."

She wondered if his nice life meant women. She couldn't imagine he had all that many free evenings where he'd sit home and watch television.

"Including going on blind dates?"

Brian grinned. "Never went on one where I was carjacked, rained on and stranded in a house that could have come from a horror movie."

Horror flashed across her face. "What have you seen?"

"I didn't have a chance to check out all the closets, so it's hard to say," he said slowly. "It's a standard hiding place for all deranged killers." He proceeded to tick off names of popular horror films that hid killers in the closet.

It took Gail a moment to realize Brian was teasing.

Once she realized what he was doing, she wasn't about to let it go without retaliation.

She didn't stop to think. Her mother would have been horrified with her reaction. At the moment, Gail didn't care. This was a night out of sync with the rest of the world, so it didn't matter.

She just launched herself at him. Not expecting her action, Brian barely had time to hold up his hands in defense. He caught her and rolled to one side before they both ended up in the fireplace. The motion ended with his lying on top of her.

Gail's eyes widened as she realized her attack backfired on her.

"Looks like I caught me something," Brian said huskily. He lazily ran his hands up and down her arms, pushing the sleeves of her sweatshirt upward.

She started to move off, then froze. There was no doubt the effect her movements were having on him.

"What do you think?" he murmured, lowering his face to hers.

"What do I think of what?" she asked, unable to breathe and not because of his weight on her. The heat of the fire warmed her side. The heat of Brian's body warmed the rest of her.

His breath feathered across her cheek with his lips following. "Think we'll get another warning from above if I try to kiss you again?" His mouth grazed hers with the fleeting touch of a butterfly on a flower. He lifted his head and cocked it to one side, listening. "I don't hear anything." He started to lower his face again.

At that moment, a faint rumble of thunder sounded in the distance. Gail rested her hand against Brian's chest stopping him from going any further.

"I don't know about you, but that sounds like a warning to me," she said softly.

"Not really." He transferred his attention to her ear. He nibbled on the top curve then along the lobe. He could feel her trembling. "Think of it more as a form of blessing." His mouth moved along her cheek and over to her mouth. By the time he reached it, her lips were already parted in anticipation.

Brian had no idea what he was expecting when he kissed Gail, but the sheer force of power that roared through him wasn't it. Nothing had ever felt so right. Her mouth moved under his in sync just as her body molded to his. Her perfume was a faint memory on her skin, but he could detect the scent of rain and smoke in her hair. Underneath them was the stronger scent of the female silently calling out to the male. It put all his senses on alert.

Gail didn't lie there passively. She surprised him by wrapping her hands around his head and kept him in place as she kissed him back. Her tongue darted inside his mouth before she teased him with playful nips along his lower lip. It was more than enough to make him hard as a rock.

"Doc, you have quite a bedside manner here," he rasped.

"Amazing, since we aren't in a bed." A throaty purr coated her words as she rotated her hips against his.

"Don't worry. I've got a good imagination." Eager to feel bare skin, he pushed his hands up under her sweatshirt. He wasn't sure whether to curse or give thanks when he realized she wasn't wearing a bra.

The flames cast a red-orange light across her face. For some reason, it sent a primitive flash through his body. Casting him back to a time when men and women could only see each other by firelight. He quickly sat up just long enough to tear his sweatshirt off and toss it to one side. As he did, he looked down at Gail. Her hair flared wild around her head, but it was her face that enraptured him.

Her delicate features were cast in shadows, but it only made her more enthralling. His stomach tightened as he thought of how that skin had felt under his touch and on his lips. It left him hungry for more. A part of him wanted to act like a barbarian and take her. But another part wanted to slowly seduce her until they were both mindless with want. The way she responded so readily to him, he didn't think *slow* would be an operative word.

"Tiring already?" she softly teased, pushing his sweatshirt up and running her hands over his chest. "I thought you service types kept in excellent shape."

He hissed when her short nails raked his nipples in a seductive circle, teasing them to hardness. "I'm not out there fighting fires, just treating people and getting them on a gurney."

"Which requires strength." She made random circles on his biceps, which bunched under her light touch. "You know, I chose you because you had the most incredible blue eyes I'd ever seen and because you looked good in a T-shirt."

Brian chuckled as he kept nibbling on her lower lip. "Nice to know I'm admired for some of my better qualities." Not wanting to leave any part of her body ignored, he pulled off her sweatshirt and pushed aside the torn edges of her dress. She looked up at him wide-eyed, and if he wasn't mistaken, a hint of apprehension shadowed her eyes. It didn't take a genius to realize some men would consider her breasts small. "It's a shame you have to cover up such a beautiful body. But then I guess if you didn't, there'd be too many men knocking down your door." The apprehension lifted as quickly as it appeared. She murmured his name when he lowered his head to caress one breast with his lips.

She tasted like a fine wine drunk at midnight. A wine that left him thirsty for more.

She arched her back when he lifted her hips to press them tightly against his erection. He wanted nothing more than to snap his fingers and make their clothes disappear.

Gail was convinced she had been transported to a magical world.

Between medical school, working crazy hours as an intern and then a resident in pediatrics, then getting her practice going, she hadn't had much time for a social life. She'd only allowed two men into her bed; both were experiences she hadn't cared to repeat. Until now.

With the fires Brian was stirring up inside her, she felt she was ready to make up for that loss.

She was so caught up in Brian's kisses, she was barely aware of her clothes leaving her body or Brian pausing long enough to loosen his trousers and kick them off. She could feel her body warming, softening for him. But even as her body lost all reason, her mind didn't.

"Wait!" Brian drew back.

"Wait?" Her shriek bounced off the walls.

His face was etched with pain. "Damn! I don't have anything with me."

Gail blinked. "I'm on the pill, but true, we have other things to consider."

Brian snapped his fingers and jumped up. Gail half sat up as she watched him run from the room. When he came back down, he knelt down beside her.

"I found more than the sweatshirts," he explained. Still, he made no move closer.

Gail realized that he was waiting for her in case she had changed her mind. She let actions give her answer as she lifted her arms.

When Brian slid inside her, she felt completed. This was like nothing she'd felt before.

With each thrust she felt herself thrown further into space. She couldn't take her eyes off Brian's face. A face now tight with desire. When he looked down at her, the flames were echoed in his eyes.

As her body tightened in response she continued looking up at him. She was positive the nova struck both of them at the same time.

BRIAN'S EYES were closed even though he couldn't sleep even if he wanted to. No, for now he was happy holding Gail. He'd had no idea there was a wild woman beneath the prim-and-proper doctor's exterior. She lay asleep with her face pressed against his chest. Her breath was warm against his skin. Enticing. Beguiling. Arousing.

The fire was starting to die down, but he didn't want to disturb her in order to throw more wood on the flames. Instead, he listened to the rain falling on the roof. In his mind, the sound was musical and soothing.

He lay there feeling his mouth curved in a contented smile. He felt so damn good! At the moment, he felt good enough to run outside and just stand there in the rain and howl. That's how good he felt.

And here he thought he was going on a date he'd be happy was over before it even started.

Who would have thought it?

GAIL'S FIRST THOUGHT was that her back and butt hurt from lying on a hard floor all night. Her next dealt with some unfamiliar, yet pleasant, aches in other parts of her body. She was covered with something soft and warm that had her thinking of just plain cuddling in it and her head was pillowed on something.

Wait a minute!

Her eyes snapped open and she looked around, taking stock of her surroundings.

A fireplace with burned wood still smoldering. A dark-green couch with a throw pillow in one corner. It appeared her head was resting on its mate. Her dress was flung across the back of the couch giving it a Christmas tree effect. Which meant... She didn't have to look under the throw to know she was nude. All she had to do was think about her skin itching from the carpet. She couldn't miss the sight of her underwear draped across the fireplace tools set.

She swallowed a moan and sat up, clutching the throw to her chest.

It wasn't a dream. She didn't have some kind of hallucination, drug-induced or not.

She grew very still, straining her ears. A faint sound came from the kitchen.

"Oh my God," she whispered, pushing her hair away from her face.

Her date for the medical association banquet started out with a carjacking and ended up with her making love with a man she barely knew.

Dr. Gail Webster, who refused to make any kind of major decision without thoroughly thinking it over, made love last night with a man she hadn't even known for twenty-four hours.

And it was good. Very good. The kind that left memories that had a woman smiling at odd times. Just as she was smiling that very minute.

"Good morning, sunshine."

She swung her gaze over in the direction of the voice. *Oh, dear.*

Brian had pulled on his tuxedo pants and nothing else. She glanced at his bare feet. His hair was tousled and he looked good enough to eat.

"The rain stopped about two hours ago," he informed her. "I thought I'd go out and see if I could find another house nearby. One that's occupied. I conducted a more thorough search of the kitchen. Sorry, no eggs or toast, but I did find some powdered orange drink in one of the cabinets."

"Good!" Her voice came out high-pitched. "Great."

Brian gave her a funny look and disappeared back into the kitchen. When he returned he carried a glass filled with orange liquid.

"Got to have your vitamins." He handed her the glass.

Gail fumbled with her cover, finally dragging it up to her chin as she took the glass from him.

"Thank you." She tried not to gag on the overly sweet taste.

"Probably something for kids," he told her. "Unfortunately, I couldn't find any instant coffee. But since there's no hot water it wouldn't have done us much good."

"This is fine," Gail assured him, valiantly finishing the drink. "I can get dressed in just a few minutes and go with you."

Brian shook his head. "Your shoes are history, darlin'. Your best bet is to stay here. Once I find a phone I'll call one of my brothers and get us some help."

"All right." She couldn't believe she sounded like a robot, but right now it was the best she could do.

He picked up his shirt and pulled it on. As he buttoned it up and tucked it into his pants, he kept his eyes on her.

"Are you all right?"

His quietly voiced question showed concern she didn't want to hear right now. She kept her gaze downcast as if the glass she held were fascinating.

When she didn't answer, he crouched down in front of her. He cupped her chin with his fingers and lifted it so she had no choice but to face him.

"Fine," she whispered. "Considering I slept on a floor all night I feel pretty good." She managed a tiny smile.

Brian's fingers lightly traced the curve of her chin. "I'll be back as soon as I can." Before she could move, he swooped down and captured her mouth.

Gail was positive the Earth tilted wildly on its axis. She held on tightly to her cover so she couldn't throw her arms around his neck and drag him back down for a repeat of last night.

As it was, Brian took his time, and when he finally pulled back, he was as breathless as she was.

"While it would be tempting to just stay here, I think I better do the right thing and play hero," he said breathlessly.

"I'll get dressed and be ready when you get back," she replied, then blushed as she realized her words could be taken more than one way. "What I mean is..."

He grinned. "Don't worry, Gail. I know what you mean. I'll be back as soon as I can."

There was no warning. Only the sense of a cool

breeze coming from the kitchen before they realized they were no longer alone.

"Why don't you two lovebirds show us your hands, and then you can tell us why you're playing house in a house you don't own."

Gail and Brian turned simultaneously to face two men wearing khaki uniforms. But it was the badges and guns the two men had in their hands that caught their attention.

Gail was the first to slowly lift her hands while somehow managing to keep the throw over her body. Brian's hands followed suit.

"We have a very good explanation," he announced.

The older of the two sheriff's deputies cast a cynical eye over their disheveled clothing. "I'm sure you do. And we'll be willing to listen to you. Just as soon as we get you over to the station."

"OF COURSE, It's only appropriate that after everything else that's happened I would be arrested," Gail moaned as she left the house.

"At least we're not in handcuffs," Brian pointed out.

"Watch your heads," the older deputy advised, placing his hand on top of Gail's head as he assisted her into the back seat of the squad car. Brian received the same treatment.

"Someone call you about us?" Brian asked as they drove off.

The younger deputy shook his head. "We were patrolling out here and saw smoke coming from the chimney."

"Too bad you weren't patrolling last night. We got caught in the storm and needed to get dry," he explained.

Gail's nose went into overdrive the moment they entered the station. She was positive the rich aroma of coffee surrounded her like rare perfume. She tried to keep close to Brian, but the deputies kept them separate.

"Would it be illegal to say I'd kill for a cup of coffee?" she murmured.

"Depends on who you plan to kill for it," Brian replied.

Gail was led into one room while Brian was taken into another. She sat down and waited. When the deputy read her her rights, she was convinced she was in major trouble. She declined asking for a lawyer. The only lawyer she knew would bust a gut laughing at her dilemma.

"Would you care to tell me why you and your boyfriend were in a house you don't own?" the man asked in a friendly voice.

"He's not my boyfriend, he's my blind date," she replied. "And we wouldn't have broken into the house if it wasn't raining. We were carjacked and dumped out there. We didn't even know where we were."

The deputy looked skeptical. "Do you really expect me to believe that?"

"But it is the truth!" she insisted.

A knock on the door sounded and another man poked his head in. He gestured for the deputy to come out.

Gail looked around the room. "No bright lights. No rubber hose," she said to herself. "And they call themselves the law."

"They have a basement for that."

She looked up and breathed a sigh of relief to see Brian enter. But her eyes lit up when she saw what he carried. Two cups of coffee.

"Oh, yes." She breathed a sigh of relief as she snatched one of the cups out of his hand. It was scalding,

it was bitter, but she didn't care. It was the heady rush
of caffeine coursing through her system she desired. She
gulped it down like water. She looked up at Brian. Without a word, he handed over the second cup.

"Damn, I thought us guys only drank coffee that
fast," he said.

"Crazy hours as an intern teaches you fast." She
drank the second cup slower.

"Dr. Roberts, do you want to file a report on the
carjacking?" the deputy following Brian asked.

"It didn't happen out here," she explained. "But
thank you for offering."

"One of my brothers is going to pick us up," Brian
told her, handing her a white bag next.

She looked inside. An eyebrow arched as she gazed
at the men. "Surprise, surprise, doughnuts."

"That's only with cops, Doc. We firemen and paramedics go for heartier fare." He grinned, grabbed a
chair and turned it around. He rested his arms on the
chair back and watched her eat.

It didn't take Brian long to realize that Gail nibbling
on a doughnut was about as sexy as her nibbling on him
last night. Her actions could have been called dainty,
but they sure aroused him.

Her hair was tousled around her shoulders, all of her
makeup was gone, and she looked about as appealing as
an unmade bed. The sweatshirt engulfed her, and now
that he could see her in the light of day, he could tell
that the color wasn't all that flattering. So why was he
itching to usher everyone out the door, lock it, and make
love to her?

He sensed his thoughts were mirrored on his face.
Gail was making an effort not to look at him, and when

she spoke to the deputy, her voice was just a little too cheerful.

He'd just have to bide his time until they were alone.

Gail showed him another side of herself last night. He was curious to find out just how many sides there were to this lady.

"I CANNOT BELIEVE you were carjacked. Damn, Brian, that sweet vehicle of yours taken!" Mark strode into the room with the force of a tornado. "How could you let someone steal your car?" He grabbed his brother by the shoulders and shook him.

"Yeah, Mark, we're both fine. Thanks for asking." Brian scowled.

"As if your sorry hide is as valuable as that car." Mark shook his head. "The guys at the station are not going to be happy about this. We had a pool going as to who would get it if anything happened to you."

"The stolen car was Gail's," Brian explained. "If you don't want to end up as dead meat, you'll just drive us home."

Mark backed up with his hands out in front of him. "Hey, watch the threats. Cops are all around us, and if they hear you, they might think you're serious."

"If they knew you better they'd understand," Brian growled, advancing on his brother.

Gail, not used to these kind of antics, slowly rose to her feet. "Please tell the owners I will return the sweatshirt after I wash it," she told the deputy.

"Mr. Walker assured us everything would be taken care of, Dr. Roberts. I guess after everything you've been through you'll be relieved to get back home," he said.

She smiled and nodded.

Brian couldn't miss that Gail was eager to leave. Considering all that had happened, he couldn't blame her.

"This is my brother, Mark, who works out of the same station I do," Brian explained. "Don't worry. The doctors told us he can't help being the way he is, so we just let him think he's normal like the rest of us."

He took her arm and guided her out of the room amid words of thanks to the deputies.

"I just want you guys to know if I ever have to be arrested, I hope it's out here. From what I saw, you've got a great jail," he joked on the way out.

"I told him I should have been the one to take you out," Mark said, helping Gail into the back seat of his utility vehicle. Both men tried to persuade her to sit in the front but she refused, saying she'd be more comfortable in the back. She almost tripped over a baseball bat as she climbed in.

Brian fixed his brother with a hard stare when he caught him staring at Gail's bare legs. "Yeah, I can see you did a great job cleaning it out. I should have called Dad."

"Right and have Mom going on about how you could have been killed." Mark sat behind the wheel and started up the engine.

Brian shot a quick look over his shoulder and caught Gail's face turning pale.

"Stuff it, Mark. The lady went through a lot last night. She's going to have enough when we start filing police reports. Okay?"

Mark glanced in the rearview mirror and realized his words were only making the situation worse.

Brian settled back in the seat and took a few deep breaths.

He needed to talk to Gail, but with Mark and his big ears there, he didn't have a chance.

He didn't believe in sleeping with a woman on their first date. But then, he'd never been on a date like this either.

Maybe he wouldn't kill Nikki for putting his picture up on that bulletin board after all.

Chapter Four

"I guess last night wasn't exactly what you expected," Gail said. She cringed as she realized just how her words sounded.

Luckily, Brian didn't take advantage of her word slip. "True, we didn't have to pretend to listen to boring speeches."

She stopped just before she reached the front door and picked up a rock. She turned it over and extracted a key from the bottom.

"Great way for thieves to get in your house," Brian commented.

"I doubt anyone would bother looking under all the rocks. Besides, thieves had my keys last night if they wanted to break in." She unlocked the door then quickly stepped inside and tapped out the code on her alarm keypad. The warning beeps stilled, and the red light turned green. "They probably had more fun with my credit cards."

Gail turned around and almost ran into Brian who stood directly behind her. She swiftly stepped back before she could touch him. She'd already learned that touching him was much too dangerous.

"I guess thank you sounds a bit much," she murmured just before she held out her hand. "But I am sorry the evening turned out the way it did." An unbidden thought of what passed between them flashed through her mind and turned her cheeks a bright pink.

Brian took her hand between the two of his. "I wouldn't say it was a total disaster," he murmured, sending another wave of color across her cheeks.

"It only happened because we were caught in a situation not of our making," she said in a low voice. She still refused to look at him. "We had our lives threatened, and then we felt we were safe, so we…" She took a deep breath. "What we did was basically celebrate the fact that we were still alive. It's a basic human function. Nothing more," she concluded in a rush.

"Basic human function," he repeated. "Yes, Doctor, I'm aware that people who have faced death will fall back on sex, but I don't think we can use that as an excuse. There was a lot more between us than celebrating our not getting killed, Gail. We were just plain hot for each other."

She tried to reclaim her hand, but he refused to release it.

"Too late to back down now, sweetheart. Oh, don't worry. I'll give you time to regain your equilibrium. After last night, there's no way I'm going to just ride off into the sunset. Nor am I going to say I'll call you and then never call," he warned her. "You owe me, Doc. You owe me that real date we missed out on last night." He cupped her face in his hands and slanted his mouth against hers.

Gail's mouth softened under his gentle pressure. She was powerless to do more than wrap her arms around him as he pulled her closer to him. It would have continued if a loud and demanding truck's horn hadn't intruded.

"Damn him," Brian muttered, stepping back. "I have to remind my parents they made a major mistake conceiving him." He dropped another kiss on her lips. "I will call you, Gail, so don't pretend to be out," he warned before running out the door. The minute he reached outside he yelled, "Knock off with the horn, will you!"

Gail closed her door and locked it. She pressed her head against the wood and stifled a moan of frustration. Her entire body quivered with minor aftershocks from Brian's kiss.

"Back to normal life," she told herself, as if invoking normal rites would calm the storm inside her. "Call the police, call a locksmith, call the credit card companies, replace my driver's license." She was already tired just thinking of the tasks ahead of her. She headed for her bedroom anticipating a hot shower and change of clothes. Maybe even a quick nap before she had to deal with real life again. "Beg the insurance company to replace my car without raising my premiums." She started shedding clothing the moment she crossed the threshold to her bedroom. Steam filled the bathroom as she turned the bathtub faucets on full blast. She poured a healthy serving of citrus-scented bath oil into the tub, and she was ready to slide into the hot water.

Before, Gail had always been able to forget the cares of the world once she was immersed in hot, scented water. With soft music playing in the background and water lapping against her chin, she could close her eyes and wander off into a fantasy world of her own. That was how she relaxed. Until now.

This time her mind didn't conjure up pictures of sun-dappled lakes or the ripple of tree-lined streams. Instead, there were flashes of hot light gilding naked flanks. Her mind echoed the murmur of a masculine voice uttering heated raw words that brought a blush to her cheeks. Instead of hot water streaming over her breasts like liquid silk, roughened fingertips traced erotic impressions across her skin. She never thought of herself as imaginative, but today, her mind went overboard with seductive images. Not even scalding water could be as hot as the visual pictures running through her mind.

Gail sat up so suddenly the water sloshed over the edge of the tub. She pressed her hands against her chest as if her effort could literally push the air out of her lungs.

"I'm not suffocating," she wheezed. "I can breathe. There's nothing wrong with me." But she still pressed her hands against her chest. When that didn't seem to help, she cupped her hands in front of her face and blew short hard breaths into them. It wasn't long before she started feeling better. She lay back in the water and swore she could hear her heart pounding furiously.

"I'm all right," she assured herself. "I will be all right. I'll use the weekend to get my life back in order."

"TELL ALL," Sheila demanded, the moment Gail entered the suite of offices through the back entrance.

"Tell all," she repeated, determined to tell as little as possible. Her promise to spend the weekend getting her life back to normal hadn't worked at all. How was she supposed to sleep if the moment she drifted off she imagined she could feel Brian lying beside her? "I picked my date up, we left for the dinner, we were carjacked, taken out to the middle of nowhere and dumped. Luckily, we found a house to stay in to get out of the rain. Of course, the next morning, two deputy sheriffs arrested us for breaking and entering.''

Gail walked into the office and dropped her purse into the bottom desk drawer. Not that there was anything important in there. The carjackers had made sure of that. ''What can I say? Just your typical date.'' She pulled on her lab coat and draped her stethoscope around her neck. She started for the door but didn't make it.

''Wait a minute!'' Sheila held up her hand à la traffic cop. ''There is no way you're getting out of here after tossing me those tasty tidbits.'' She steered Gail back to her desk chair and pushed her into it.

''I have patients!''

''Not for another hour.''

''I need coffee.''

''You can have your coffee after you tell me everything.''

Gail rolled her eyes. ''Remind me again why I hired you.''

Sheila smirked. ''Because I'm the best.''

Gail fixed her with a level stare. ''If I was going to hire the best, I would have hired the P.A. who looked like Harrison Ford.''

''Damn, I would have hired him too,'' she admitted. ''Okay, no more excuses. I want all the details.''

Gail took a deep breath. She knew she would have to say it all at once or she'd find a way to put off the persistent woman. ''My date suggested I not take the freeway because traffic was heavy at that hour. As a result, these two creeps forced me at gunpoint to drive out of the city. They dumped us, kept the car, my purse, my date's wallet. We tried walking for help, got caught in a rainstorm and were lucky enough to find someone's vacation house. My date broke in and since there was no electricity, made a fire so we could dry out. The next morning—"

"You spent the night together?"

She cast her a dry look. "There wasn't exactly a bus stop in the vicinity." There was no way she would tell her physician's assistant just how they spent the night. "The next morning, my date was going out to see if he could find a phone. Instead, two deputy sheriffs showed up, thought we'd broken in to rob the place, and took us down to the station. My date straightened everything out, called his brother who picked us up and drove us home. I spent the weekend reporting my car stolen, making calls to cancel my credit cards, and today I'm going to replace my driver's license and pick up the rental car the insurance company is providing for me."

"Oh, honey." Sheila pulled her out of her chair and hugged her tightly. "What a nightmare that must have been for you!"

By now, Gail should have been used to Sheila's spontaneous displays of affection. Raised by parents who didn't believe in showing their emotions, she wasn't used to someone hugging her just to make her feel better. Eighteen months with Sheila, who hugged her just because it was a pretty day, had quickly taught her different. At first, she had stiffened every time Sheila hugged her. Now, she was getting used to it. And sometimes, she even found solace in Sheila's hugs.

"They took my beautiful new car, Sheila," she murmured, hating to hear her self-pity. "And my favorite lipstick was in my purse. My new shoes gave me blisters, and my dress was ruined by the rain." *And I did something so crazy you wouldn't believe it if I told you. I made incredible love with an even more incredible guy.* "Brian said after the carjackers had their fun driving the car it would end up in a chop shop.'' Her lower lip quivered. "A chop shop is where car thieves tear your car into pieces and sell the parts. It hadn't even had its first oil change.''

Sheila's eyes darkened with sympathy. "Not exactly the kind of weekend I'd hoped for you." She bunched her hair in one hand and expertly braided it in no time, securing it off with a red elastic band. "Are you sure you want to work today?''

"I'm fine. Besides today's a full day, and the last thing we want to do is reschedule all those patients. Sheila?'' Gail spoke slowly. "May I have my coffee now?''

Sheila put her arm around her shoulders and steered her out of the office. "Honey, not only can you have your coffee you can have a doughnut, too.''

Sheila hadn't expected Gail to suddenly burst out laughing.

"SO YOU'RE NOT going to tell me anything, are you?''

"Not a thing.''

"She didn't look like something the dog would refuse for dinner, so something must have happened,'' Mark persisted.

Brian sat back in his chair until the front two legs lifted off the floor. Ever since he and his brother reported for work that morning, Mark had done his best to find out exactly what happened between him and Gail. Brian would have preferred time to himself to think back over that night but no such luck. He thought he and Gail had acted pretty impersonal on the way back, but there must have been something Mark picked up on.

"Yeah, something happened. The guy at the tux rental shop told me I'd have to pay for the tux. Said it must have been some party," he growled. "I even showed him a copy of the police report I filed on my stolen wallet, but he didn't care. He said my wallet getting stolen and getting caught in the rain in the tux were two different things. I'll tell you one thing. I'm not going to that shop again."

"Again, huh?" Mark grinned. "That mean you're taking the cute doctor out again? True, the two of you have a lot in common. Both in the medical field. Both driving hot cars. Man, am I relieved those guys didn't take your 'Vette. Now, that would have been a crime."

"Amen to that," Kurt Anderson, one of the firemen walked into the kitchen and dropped onto the leather couch set under a window and facing the television set. Several other men were already there watching Cartoon Network. "You still haven't told us who would get the car if something happened to you. An accident can happen at any time." He flashed the boyish grin that brought more than one woman to his side.

"I'll make sure I stay away from you when you're holding a sharp object," Brian retorted. "You guys are animals."

"And proud of it!' Kurt started howling and others joined in.

Brian leaned forward so the chair's front legs could settle on the floor. "I'm better off with a dog."

"Think your sister would put my picture up on that bulletin board, so I could get lucky, too?" one of the men called after him.

"I can't imagine any woman being that desperate." Brian walked out front. The station doors were open so the fire trucks could be washed. Boots, a chocolate lab, and the station mascot, lay on the concrete enjoying the morning sun. Brian guessed the dog had no idea he was next in line to be washed. Otherwise, he'd be trying to hide under the bunks. For a breed that was supposed to love water, Boots tended to avoid baths as much as a cat would.

Brian snagged a chair and dragged it out into the sun. He sat down with his legs stretched out in front of him, and his crossed hands rested on his stomach.

"Working on your tan, Walker?" one of the men washing the truck joked.

"Nah, I came out to watch you guys chase Boots around when it's his turn."

Brian knew enough not to say the *B* word since Boots tended to run and try to hide in ingenious places to escape a bath. Everyone's fervent wish was that the alarm wouldn't go off once the dog was lathered up.

Brian squinted against the sun but felt too lazy to go back in for his sunglasses.

He'd wanted to call Gail all weekend, but he wasn't sure she would be ready to talk to him. He was hoping if he gave her a few days, she'd be more amiable. She'd looked pretty spooked when he left her. If his brother hadn't been waiting for him, he would have stayed and insisted they talk about the previous night. Instead, for the past two days, he'd done the talking inside his head. Too bad she hadn't been there to hear him.

Brian had started the date wishing it were over before it started. He had no idea one night would change his life. He wasn't sure how it happened. Only that it did. Now he was craving to see her again.

He learned that Gail was easy to talk to, funny and stirred something inside him. Not just his libido. Sure, she did that, and more. Now he wanted to find out more than just how she kissed and felt in his arms.

His body tightened at the memory. She'd smelled of rain and the faint scent of perfume.

Should he send her roses? Or some other kind of flowers?

They'd made love, but did that mean she'd go out with him again?

She hadn't turned back into that uptight woman he'd met that first time, had she?

He started laughing when two men hoisted a flailing and howling Boots into a large metal washtub. It wasn't long before they were as wet and sudsy as the dog.

And, as fate would have it, the alarm sounded. Brian tucked thoughts of Gail into the back of his mind and raced inside.

Time to go to work.

"Now, those are what I call flowers," Sheila declared, standing back to admire the floral arrangement that had just been delivered.

"This is much more romantic than roses," Lora, the receptionist, announced. "And they're for Dr. Roberts." She gestured with a long, bright, coral-polished nail to the small white card tucked among the colorful blossoms. She tucked a wayward strand of golden blond hair behind her ear. With colorful bands keeping her shoulder-length hair back and the simplicity in her wardrobe, twenty-two-year-old Lora had an Alice in Wonderland air about her. And more men in her life than any one woman needed.

"Oh, really?" Sheila's eyes lit up with avid curiosity.

"Who got them this time?" Gail asked, walking up. With three single nurses, female doctors, physician's assistant and receptionist, flowers were seen on the front desk almost on a daily basis.

"They're for you, Dr. Roberts." Lora beamed, looking as if her beloved child had just done something brilliant. In this case, it was almost true. This was the first time flowers had been delivered to Gail.

"Amazing. I've never had a disastrous date send me flowers," Sheila murmured.

Gail didn't reply. She was too busy admiring the assortment of wildly colored blooms. She plucked the white envelope out of its niche and tucked it into the pocket of her lab coat. She'd read it later.

"No, they can't be for me," Moira Blake, one of the other doctors, commented. She dropped a file on the desk and picked up pink phone messages marked with her name. "Stephen wouldn't send anything less than roses."

Sheila nudged Gail, but Gail ignored her. Moira had been a thorn in her side since Moira's first day with the medical center six months ago. Lovely, self-assured, and confident to the point of putting off the women around her, Moira was the stuff that didn't make friends. Everyone wondered how she could have a successful psychological therapy practice when as a human being she was truly miserable.

Gail silently gnashed her teeth and fixed a smile on her lips. "Actually, Moira, they're for me, and I like the idea that the person who sent them to me had an original thought."

Sheila stood behind Moira. She licked her finger and traced a vertical line in the air. One for Gail's side.

Moira's smile didn't come anywhere near her eyes. "Roses are the language of romance. But then, Gail, I guess *romance* isn't a word in your vocabulary, is it?"

Gail thought about the night spent with Brian. She'd tried to tell herself that it was nothing more than the heat of the moment. Lust, pure and simple. But there was much more to it, a part of her argued. She just didn't want to admit it.

"Perhaps I just prefer not to talk about it," she said softly before walking away. But not without seeing Sheila mark the air with another vertical line.

At that moment, Gail felt pretty damn good.

It wasn't long before she felt even better.

"I was just going to call you," she told Brian when she was informed he was on the phone for her. "Thank you for the flowers. You didn't have to." She briefly touched the note resting inside her lab coat pocket. *Any date that begins with a carjacking and ends with a near arrest couldn't be all bad. Want to try again?*

"Does that mean you're willing to give it another try?" he asked. "Of course, I'd have to find another tux rental shop. Amazing how disagreeable some guys get just because their merchandise comes back a little worse for wear."

Her laughter erupted before she could stop it.

"Is that a yes?" he asked, encouraged by her laughter. "Come on, Gail. Maybe I can't promise you that gourmet meal and award, but I can promise a nice evening out. I'm on duty for a few days but would be free this weekend. Come on, Gail, say yes," he coaxed.

She could feel that suffocation feeling taking over again. How much of that past date was he willing to ignore, and how much did he want to recreate?

"Just dinner, maybe some dancing if you'd like," he said quietly, apparently guessing the direction of her thoughts.

Stay home with a good book or the latest AMA journal.

Sound advice in her mind.

Good thing it stayed there.

"Saturday night," she said before she could change her mind.

"Saturday night," he repeated. "I'll pick you up. And don't worry, it won't be the truck." Another uncanny foray into her mind.

"Maybe we'd be safer in it. I can't imagine anyone would want to carjack that truck."

His answering laughter sent way too many warm fuzzy feelings through her.

"Sweetheart, they would be drooling buckets if they knew what kind of engine that truck had." Alarms suddenly sounded in the background. "Got to go. I'll see you at seven."

Gail hung up. She again fingered the card in her pocket. It was still there, not a figment of her imagination.

Moira's earlier words had stung. Romance hadn't been something Gail had hoped for. The few relationships she'd been in had turned out disastrous. Not that she ever advertised it. She preferred keeping her mistakes to herself. Actually, she kept to herself, period.

Gail was aware she grew up as an introvert. She'd been a surprise in her parents' later years of life. They were intellectuals who didn't know what to do with a child. So they sat her down with books and urged her to keep her world within those confines.

No wonder she graduated from high school two years ahead of her age group. Even if her parents were disappointed she hadn't graduated three years ahead of schedule. If she felt out of her depth in high school, it was more keenly felt in college and later in medical school.

She picked up the file folder for her next patient.

She wasn't going to think about her date this weekend. Not think about what she'd wear, wonder where they'd go.

She wasn't even going to think about the man who looked so dapper in a tuxedo but had the nerve to wear vivid-purple boxer shorts under it.

Chapter Five

This time Gail wasn't taking any chances. She'd owned her black crepe dress with the sweetheart neckline for two years. Her black silk heels were dressy but also very comfortable. She pulled her hair up into a simple twist with a minimum of mousse and hair spray.

Was it a good idea for her to go out with Brian again?

Look what happened last time.

Her stomach muscles clenched, a sure sign she was nervous. She'd spent the night before every exam in the bathroom throwing up. So far she hadn't suffered that calamity, but she feared it would appear if she wasn't careful.

"We had a bad date that completely skewed our perception of each other. Tonight will be a perfectly ordinary evening," she told her mirrored reflection as she applied lipstick. She quickly realized it wasn't a good idea to talk out loud while applying lipstick. When her doorbell rang, the tube almost went flying against the mirror.

She wiped her hands down the sides of her dress and headed for the front door.

It was a scene straight out of a movie.

"Gail." Brian bowed slightly as he presented her with a long-stemmed rose. Instead of the usual red, this one was a shade of soft peach that looked luminous in the twilight. She held it against her nose and inhaled the seductive scent.

"It's lovely," she murmured, able to easily hold the rose since the thorns had been removed. "Thank you."

"When I saw it, I knew it was meant for you. It looked and felt like your skin." His voice lowered to a provocative rumble as he guided her down the walkway.

"I didn't think hothouse roses held a scent."

"They do if they come from my mom's garden." He grinned.

Gail looked past him and did a double take at the sight of the black limousine waiting at the curb. A man dressed in a dark suit and white shirt stood by the open door. He smiled and tipped his head in greeting as Brian guided her inside.

"He's a cop who works as a chauffeur when he's off duty," Brian explained as he settled in beside her on the luxurious leather upholstery. "I dare anyone to try to carjack him and survive to tell the tale. I also checked the weather report. No rain."

She shook her head, amazed at his foresight.

"You weren't taking any chances, were you?"

"Not a one." He pulled a bottle of champagne out of the ice bucket and poured two glasses, handing one to Gail. "The only way to drink and drive," he told her, touching his glass against hers in a toast.

"I did not expect this," she confessed, sipping the sparkling liquid.

"I figured we needed a special treat after last weekend." He stretched his legs out. "So tell me, Doc, how was your week? Find any strange munchkin ailments?"

"Nothing exotic unless you count the little boy who came in with a toy truck Super Glued to his butt." She held up her hand. "Don't even ask me how it got there. I hated asking. But I can tell you that his younger sister has lost computer and television privileges for the next month."

"Sounds like my family. When my older sister was ten she decided she wanted to be a hairdresser. She used me for practice. I was so cheap back then. Promise me a candy bar, and I was your friend for life. I ended up with very smelly orange curls courtesy of a home perm and hair color. She was grounded for two months, and I had to go to school with orange hair until it grew out. I thought about cutting all my hair down to my scalp but realized it wouldn't do any good. It was orange, too."

"I bet your family doctor loved your family," she said, holding the champagne glass between her fingertips.

"He once told my mom that we kids sent his through college and law school," Brian said with a sense of pride. "I think we paid for his wife's face-lift, too, but I guess he wouldn't want that known."

Gail nodded. "I have patients like that. I always see them as a challenge."

"Ever wonder how they'll turn out?" Brian asked. "Whether they'll end up as model citizens or one of the most wanted. Nobel Prize winners or famous film star."

She agreed she had.

"So, what got you into pediatrics and not some fancy speciality like dermatology or plastic surgery?" he asked, picking up the bottle and pouring her a little more champagne.

"The rotation I enjoyed the most was pediatrics," she

replied. "To be honest, I didn't think I had the patience to treat kids. I was an only child and wasn't around other children except at school. Surprisingly, I discovered that my lack of time around children didn't hinder my medical skills." She placed her glass in the hollowed-out area of the console meant for glassware. "The medical center was looking for a pediatrician at the time I was looking around, and I took the position."

"The medical center's strictly pediatrics, right?"

She nodded. "We offer all pediatric specialities including a dentist and psychologist."

"One-stop shopping," Brian quipped.

"I wouldn't exactly put it that way," Gail said dryly. She glanced out the smoked window when the vehicle started to slow to a stop. "I don't see any men with guns."

"Always a good way to begin the evening." Brian stepped out when the door opened. He turned to offer his hand to Gail.

As she stretched one leg out, the slit in her dress parted to reveal a shapely thigh encased in a black sheer stocking. She glanced up and didn't miss Brian's gaze fastened on her leg. She couldn't stop the blush working its way up her throat. When she straightened up, he curved his arm around her waist.

"I think I found a better way to begin the evening," he murmured in her ear as they walked toward the entrance of the restaurant.

Gail's eyes widened as she looked around at the interior as the maître d' led them to their curved booth. Brian slid in next to her, his thigh touching hers.

She opened her menu and took one look at the offerings. She worried when she couldn't find any prices.

"Brian, no offense," she whispered, afraid of being overheard, "but this place looks very expensive."

"Don't worry, Gail. My dad keeps the owner's three classic T-Birds running, and the family gets prime tables." He proceeded to make suggestions then looked up and smiled when their waiter appeared.

Gail listened in fascination as Brian struck up a conversation with the waiter. She'd been in restaurants like this where the waiters were snootier than the diners. But then there was Brian who obviously didn't understand the word *stranger*.

With Gail's permission, Brian consulted the waiter for recommendations, and it wasn't long before a bottle of wine and their appetizers arrived.

Gail thought of the courses ahead of them and wished she'd worn a looser dress.

"Now comes the interrogation." Brian figuratively rubbed his hands with glee.

Gail enjoyed foreign films.

Brian liked action and adventure.

Gail read popular fiction.

Brian preferred psychological thrillers and suspense.

Gail spent her days off at art galleries and out-of-the-way shops offering curios.

Brian wasn't into shopping, but when he went, he liked flea markets.

She played golf and tennis. Brian teased her about doctors and their golf games.

He was happy playing touch football with his brothers and friends.

Gail enjoyed dressing up for an evening out for a concert or dinner even if those times seemed to be rare.

Brian's idea of an evening out was watching sports

or shooting pool at a tavern frequented by fellow paramedics and firemen.

He offered the fact he slept in a T-shirt and pajama bottoms, but Gail declined to offer her choice of sleeping apparel.

The evening was leisurely as they ate and shared their likes and dislikes.

With each word they spoke, it became more and more clear that they were complete opposites. They couldn't find one thing in common.

Even down to Gail loving spinach and Brian thinking it belonged in Popeye cartoons.

She wasn't looking for a relationship. She didn't have time for one! She'd only contacted Brian because she needed a date for the dinner that she didn't end up attending anyway.

Brian was feeling the need to nest, so to speak. The idea of having a family of his own was sounding better all the time.

What did they have to talk about, anyway?

BRIAN KNEW it didn't take a genius to realize they had nothing in common. So, how did dinner pass by so quickly as they discussed their likes and dislikes?

They should have had nothing to talk about. They should each be discreetly glancing at their watches or pagers with hopes of cutting the evening short.

Other than Gail explaining the nuances of the latest film she saw, which Brian was convinced he would have slept through. And Brian enthusiastically explaining the finer points of football, which had Gail's eyes glazing over.

As for the Internet, Gail only used it to seek out medical information and correspond with colleagues. For

Brian, it was the perfect playground to find just about anything and everything.

So why did the time seem to fly? Was it because they barely stopped talking? Or because neither could seem to stop looking into each other's eyes. Their time spent in the restaurant doubled and even then they felt reluctant to leave. Instead, they lingered over their coffee.

GAIL WAS RELIEVED the evening went so well. She was right, the other time was one of those flukes. She could go home with a clear conscience. Right after she informed Brian she wouldn't see him again.

Even though the night was chilly, the limousine's interior was warm as Brian ushered Gail inside.

"This was a wonderful evening, Brian," she began, angling on the seat so she could face him.

He smiled. "I'm glad you think so," he murmured, catching a stray curl between his fingertips. "I like this hairstyle better than the last one. It's more touchable." He wrapped a wisp of hair around his finger.

Her breath hitched in her throat. "No mousse or hair spray," she said, without knowing why she would offer the information.

"That's why I only detect your perfume." His mouth was perilously close to hers. "Did I tell you how much I like your perfume?"

She tried to push against his shoulders as she glanced wildly at the smoked-glass partition dividing the driver from them.

"Brian!"

"He can't see anything." He picked up the peach rose and brushed it against the soft underside of her throat with his lips following. "He's a professional. Knows his place and all that."

She tried valiantly to gather her wits, which wasn't easy considering what Brian was doing to her. Not once had his hands strayed below the waist. In fact, his hands cupped her face as he trailed his lips across the curve of her cheek and back toward her ear.

"I'm sure you see there's too many differences between us," she managed to state amid gasps each time his mouth caressed another tender spot. She shivered and not because she was cold. "I'm sorry, Brian, you're a really nice guy."

"That's me. Mr. Congeniality. Nice earrings, by the way." He curled his tongue around the gold filigree.

Her head was spinning and she had nothing to blame it on. "It's just that—" her fingers clenched the lapels of his jacket. She felt she had to or she'd fall.

"Wait a second, honey." He loosened her fingers and leaned back long enough to shrug out of his jacket. He tossed it onto the seat across from them.

Even as she spoke, her hands immediately returned to the crisp white shirt that covered warm skin.

"We're just so different," she babbled, loosening first his tie then two shirt buttons and sliding her fingers inside. "We have different tastes."

"You taste just fine to me." He nibbled on her ear. "Better than fine. And feel better."

Gail almost slid off the seat in a puddle of want when Brian trailed his hand along her thigh.

"So, you don't think we should try to see each other again," he murmured.

She should have breathed a sigh of relief when his hand stopped just above her knee, but breathing wasn't something she was thinking about at the moment. Not when Brian finally settled on caressing her mouth.

She was drowning and not regretting it, either. Not as

long as Brian was kissing her the way he was and holding her the way he was. She should have remembered that his kisses seemed to have a narcotic effect on her. Just one wasn't enough. It didn't matter because more were coming.

If Gail had stretched out on the comfortable seat, she wasn't aware of it. If Brian had stretched out beside her, she wasn't aware of that, either. She was too engrossed in the emotions swirling through her with each nibble on her lips, with each sweep of his tongue around hers and each heated murmur in her ear.

"There—" she gasped as she felt his featherlight touch graze her nipples. They immediately tightened under his caress. "There has to be more than a physical attraction between two people. They have to be able to converse on an intellectual level. Have common interests." She moaned softly when he traced a line between fabric and skin. "And we—"

"Don't seem to have either." He finished her sentence for her in a much too agreeable tone to her hazy mind.

"That's right," she said, feeling her mind swim around in circles. His mouth returned to hers with a hunger that she reciprocated. She clutched at his shoulders, holding him against her because she couldn't find the will to let go.

"You were saying?" Brian asked, pushing aside her hair to plant kisses along her temple.

"Saying?" she asked vaguely. *She was saying something? What could she have said to him?*

"How incompatible we are." He nuzzled the sensitive area just behind her ear.

"Brian!" Gail fought to reach the surface of her senses. A tiny voice reminded her of what she'd been taught by a former medical school classmate in case she needed to defend herself. She reached for his crotch with a firm hand. Except the reaction wasn't what she'd expected!

He grinned. "I guess we're pretty compatible after all."

Gail snatched her hand back as if it had been burned. "That's not what I meant and you know it!"

Even when Brian drew back, she couldn't immediately regain her senses. She sat up, pulling her skirt down over her knees. It wasn't until then she realized that the limo was no longer moving. She looked out the window and discovered they were parked in front of her house.

She wasn't sure whether to be mortified or relieved. How long had they been parked there?

It was a few more minutes before the car door opened. Brian climbed out and helped Gail out. He kept her arm tucked in his as they walked up to the front door. When she looked blankly at the door, he took her purse out of her hand and opened it, easily finding her key ring. Within moments, the door was unlocked and open. Gail recovered her wits in time to disarm her alarm.

"Thank you for a lovely evening." When in doubt, fall back on parental teaching. "I'm just sorry things turned out the way they did." Considering what had been going on just minutes before, holding out her hand didn't seem right, but she did it anyway.

Brian smiled and enveloped her hand between his. "I'm sorry we didn't have more time, too."

Gail was ready to blast him but good, but before she got a word out she noticed the wicked twinkle in his eye. She closed her mouth then opened it again.

"Then you can understand it isn't you personally,"

she said primly. "We knew during our first meeting that the dinner would be the only time we would see each other. Considering the number of women going to the spa, I'm sure your phone will always be busy." There. She'd recovered her wits and sounded more like herself now. She tamped down the tiny voice reminding her she'd taken down his picture and phone number. She silently vowed to replace it the next time she went in there. "I'm glad you understand."

Brian's smile didn't slip, and his expression didn't tell her a thing. He kept her hand warmly covered by his. He tilted his head and pressed a kiss against her cheek.

"Get a good night's sleep, Gail," he advised. "I'll try to call you before I go back on duty." He released her hand and walked back to the waiting limo.

She shook herself. "Wait a minute! Brian, I told you I wouldn't see you again!"

He turned around and waved. "One word of advice, sweetheart," he called back. "Wait until you're asked."

Gail could only stand there dumbstruck as she watched the limo glide away. She felt as if she were slinking inside her own house. Or hiding.

Gail's relationships hadn't been many but she knew even if it had been one or a hundred and one, she still wouldn't have come across a man like Brian Walker. He was definitely one of a kind.

"No problem," she decided, going into her bedroom. "I just have to refuse to take his calls. He'll get the message soon enough."

"So TELL ME, Lora, what's her excuse for not taking my call today?" Brian asked. Holding his cordless phone against one ear, he could circle the backyard. He winced at the height of the grass. It should have been mowed a week ago. He'd have to do it today before he left for the station.

"She's with a patient right now, Mr. Walker. Would you like to leave a message?" the receptionist chirped.

He grinned. "I get it. She's standing right there, isn't she?"

"That's right."

His grin grew even broader. "Just tell her she can't hide from me once I'm off duty again."

"I will relay that for you, Mr. Walker. Thank you for calling."

Brian disconnected the call and set the phone on the patio table. Another wince. He'd meant to clean the metal surface and paint it a month ago. Right about the same time that Gail started avoiding him like the plague.

"Sorry, Jeff. Can't help you fix the fence today because I've got yard work to do." A voice sounded from the side.

Brian turned around to face a man who looked remarkably like him. "That's right. Yard work." He bent down and pulled up a weed, holding it high as proof.

Jeff Walker, Brian's brother older by two years sauntered across the lawn. "Yeah, that is rough work. I hope you realize you disappointed your two nieces by not showing up. I guess they thought you'd be coming over there to play with them instead of working with me."

"That's because they're cuter than you. But then, the entire world is cuter than you," Brian joked. "

Jeff shook his head. "Are you ever going to do anything responsibly?"

"When I'm old and gray." Brian swept up his phone and carried it into the house. "Then I'll become a regular Jim Anderson," he said, naming the lead character in *Father Knows Best.* "The entire family will look upon me as a regular oracle."

"Right, just as soon as the sun rises in the west and Kansas ends up as oceanfront property," Jeff jeered as he followed him inside. "You're having too much fun being a kid who gets to follow fire trucks for a living."

"So says the man who drives a fire truck for a living." Brian reminded him, as he opened the refrigerator door and snagged two bottles of Coke. He handed one to Jeff and gestured to a chair. His yard might have been in need of some TLC, but at least his kitchen was neat and tidy.

"Yeah, along with having a wife, two kids, another on the way and a mortgage," Jeff twisted the top off and tossed it toward the wastebasket making a perfect two-point drop.

"That's because you found the perfect woman the first time around. You and Abby laid eyes on each other, and you two could barely wait to get hitched. Since then, all you guys do is make babies. I'm just glad you make cute babies. I've seen some who are downright ugly."

Jeff grinned, a replica of his own brother's grin. "Sure they're cute. They look like their dad."

"Wrong, bro. They're cute 'cuz they look like their mama." Brian took a deep swallow of the cold liquid. "Her brains too, thank God."

"Look who's talking about brains. I'm not the one calling a certain woman doctor on a daily basis and hearing every excuse in the book why she won't talk to you. Too bad. As a pediatrician, she'd be familiar with your age range."

"Pediatrician." Brian's gaze grew unfocused. He slowly swiveled his head and looked at his brother.

"Didn't you tell me Abby wanted to find a new pediatrician?"

Jeff was only too familiar with his brother's schemes. "No."

"I happen to know of one who received recognition from her peers. Someone who's responsible." *Smells like heaven and kisses like sin. Someone who feels just right in a man's arms.* He didn't mention those facts to his brother. Jeff and Abby took their children's health care seriously. "Someone who has the children's interests at heart."

Jeff just sat there, tipping the bottle upward and drinking deeply.

Brian kept his own bottle twirling between his fingertips. He was used to his brother's silences. He finished his Coke and took the bottle over to the sink, rinsing it out and tossing it into the recycling bin. He took Jeff's bottle and did the same.

"Abby has the last word in choosing the girls' doctors," was all Jeff said.

"Thought you were the boss of that family." Brian couldn't resist a little tweak of the male ego.

His brother didn't rise to the bait. "Abby's boss of what she does best and I'm boss of what I do best."

Brian rolled his eyes. "Good thing Dad's not hearing this. He'd be sick to his stomach."

"Doubt it." Jeff grinned. "Look, you want Abby to take the girls to this doctor, you talk to her. Course, she'd tell you that still might not get you into the lady's good graces. What the hell did you do to tick her off, anyway?"

Made love with her in a way that made angels weep. Brian chose not to share that tidbit with his brother. That was something he preferred to keep to himself.

Besides, he was still trying to figure out how she could think they were incompatible after the way they practically explode when they're around each other. Good thing he knew how to convince her otherwise.

GAIL WAS CONVINCED she would die at any moment.

"What makes you think you don't have the flu?" Doug Carter challenged when he caught her coming out of the rest room. "All you have to do is look in our waiting room to see it's going around."

"I went out to dinner with friends last night and had shrimp bisque. I think it was that," she replied, making her way into her office.

He paused in her office doorway. "What about the night before? You've had this for the past couple days, kid. Your best bet would be to go home and go to bed and get this bug out of your system. No use in your giving it to your healthy patients," he advised, as he walked away.

Gail knew he was right, but she didn't feel as if she had the flu that was going around lately.

"I'll be fine in a couple minutes. I don't have any other symptoms, and I haven't been eating all that good lately." She smiled when Sheila, bearing a steaming cup, entered.

"Ginger tea. Perfect for a rolling tummy," Sheila announced, setting the cup down on Gail's desk then hopping up to perch on the corner. "Drink up."

She cautiously sipped the hot liquid and soon felt her stomach calming.

"No more shrimp bisque for me," she insisted. "All I had to do was get up this morning, and I could feel it coming back to smack me in the face."

Sheila jerked her head to indicate to Gail not to stop

drinking. "This hasn't been the first morning it's happened for you, Gail? Are you sure you're not telling us something?" Her gaze bored into her boss's eyes.

"Not telling you something? Like what? That I drank expired milk or something?" Gail's laughter stilled under Sheila's unwavering gaze. She still displayed mild confusion over the woman's words. "What?"

"And you call yourself a doctor?"

"Fine, Sheila, you're having a joke at my expense. I'm glad I amuse you so much. Why don't you go give a shot or something." She grumpily waved her away.

Sheila hopped off the desk and headed for the door. Just as she started to open it, she looked back over her shoulder. "By the way, Gail. When was your last period?" She didn't bother to wait for a reply but sauntered out.

Gail wasn't even aware her coffee mug fell to the floor. Once she recovered from her shock, she grabbed her calendar and did some backtracking. After she counted back, she did it back again. And a third time. She would have done it a fourth, but she knew it wouldn't matter. The results would still be the same.

"There's no way. None at all," she whispered. "It's a bug. Something caused by the stress of too much work. The flu coming on." She didn't add that it was all lack of sleep because every time she fell asleep she dreamed of Brian Walker.

She still refused to take his calls. And ignored her co-workers teasing her about her ardent admirer.

Now she feared she was facing something she couldn't so easily ignore in the hope it would go away.

"Hey, Walker, you've got a phone call," one of the men's voices rang out.

Brian, who'd been playing basketball with some of the other men behind the fire station, tossed the ball in the air and loped inside.

"Walker," he said, wiping his sweaty face with the tail of his T-shirt.

"Brian. It's Gail Roberts."

He didn't need clarification to know the identity of his caller. He'd been hearing that voice in his dreams just about every night.

"Is this a bad time?" She misunderstood his silence.

"No, this is fine. I was just out playing basketball," he explained. "How are you?" Funny, he could have sworn he heard a muffled sob. "Gail?"

"Fine, just fine. Ah, the reason I was calling was to see if you could come to dinner. I wasn't sure what your schedule was or if you'd even like to come or—"

"This Saturday?" He didn't waste any time.

"That's fine. About six?"

Her formal tone made him curious because he was positive he heard uncertainty in her voice. "I'll be there."

"Good. I'll see you then."

Chapter Six

It should be easy.

All she has to do is serve him dinner. Relax him with good food and maybe a nice wine and then drop the bomb.

Brian, I'm pregnant.

That's all she'd have to do.

Except Gail wasn't a good cook, not even passable. Brian wasn't all that fond of wine, and she was never good about dropping bombs.

She'd only known the truth for a good ten minutes before she knew she would have to tell Brian. They occupied different parts of town and different life-styles. She might have told him she didn't want to see him again, but he was going to be a father, and she knew it was only fair he knew about the baby.

Gail knew how much Brian loved his nieces and nephews, and his love for kids in general. She couldn't keep him from his child. She wanted the baby to know both parents.

Green salad, chicken breasts for the barbecue, potatoes baking in the oven, and rolls ready to pop in the oven. She purchased an apple pie for dessert.

She felt better once she heard the doorbell ring.

"Hi there," Brian greeted her with a grin and kiss on the cheek. He walked in as if he belonged there. "I know you're not too keen on beer so I brought some wine." He held up a paper bag.

"Thank you." She took the bag from him. "I knew you preferred beer, so I picked some up for you. Would you like one now?"

"Sure." He followed her, intrigued by the enticing sight of her gently swaying hips as she walked into the kitchen. She was informally dressed in navy linen shorts and a pink polo shirt with her hair pulled up into a ponytail. He would have preferred seeing her out of both. He wanted to see her looking mussed.

"I thought we could eat on the patio," she told him as she pulled a bottle of beer out of the refrigerator and a glass out of the freezer. "I have some chicken for the barbecue and potatoes baking. It won't take long."

"Sounds good to me. No need to dirty a glass." He took the bottle out of her hand. "Anything I can do to help?"

"There's dressing in the refrigerator." She picked up the salad bowl.

Brian helped her carry out the food and offered to cook the chicken.

"It might be a good idea if you did. I've been known to burn food on that thing rather than cook it," she confessed.

"Ah, it's easy. Just watch the master," he advised, picking up the platter holding the chicken.

Brian grinned as he noticed Gail's concentration as he cooked the chicken. There was no missing the tiny furrow between her brows as she watched his every move. He also didn't miss that she watched him just as closely. But every time she found him looking at her, she looked away. If he wasn't mistaken he'd swear she was nervous.

The cool and composed Dr. Gail Roberts was nervous? He would have sworn she didn't have one nervous bone in her body.

Of course, she acted a little out of character when she asked him to accompany her to that banquet. But things have changed since then.

He'd seen her naked!

A picture of her flushed features lit golden from firelight flashed through his mind.

He thought of the fireplace he saw in the family room attached to the kitchen. So the evening was a little warm. They could always turn on the air-conditioning.

"How has your work been going?" she asked, as they served themselves the golden-brown chicken.

"Busy. The usual. Heart attacks, automobile accidents, a kid stuck in a toilet." Once hearing her laughter at the latter, he continued with his story. "His sister told him he takes too long and he told her fine, he'd just live in the toilet. He somehow folded himself up, but once in he discovered he couldn't get out. His parents weren't too happy with him."

Gail kept on laughing, waving a hand across her face.

"He's one of my patients," she giggled. "I saw Teddy at the hospital. He was so impressed with the firemen who got him out and the paramedics who took care of him that he intends to be both when he grows up."

"And here I figured he'd always be the one to get into trouble."

"He will be," she assured him. "But he's also a charmer."

"Surprising our work parallels so much," he commented. "Who would have thought?"

She offered a wan smile. "Yes, who would have?"

Having so many brothers and sisters taught Brian early on how to tell if someone was hiding something. There was no doubt in his mind that Gail was hiding something very big.

"Come on, Gail. Out with it. Why after all the times you've turned me down for dinner, you invite me over tonight."

She carefully set her fork and knife on the side of her plate and laced her fingers together on top of the table.

"At first, I wasn't sure I would even tell you this," she began. "But then sanity prevailed, and I realized I should tell you."

Brian held up his hands to stop her flow of words. "I'm glad to see you're getting to the point, Gail. What, you need a statement about your car for your insurance company? No problem. You didn't need to invite me over for dinner. All you had to do was ask."

"That's not it." She looked a bit desperate.

"Then what do you need? Blood? A kidney?" he joked.

Gail stood up so fast, the table shook and her plate fell off the edge.

"I'm pregnant!"

It was to Brian's misfortune he happened to have popped a radish in his mouth at the time she made her announcement. His face immediately turned purple, and he coughed violently.

"Oh, no!" Gail ran over to him and pounded hard on his back. He choked once, and the errant slice flew out of his mouth. He grabbed the side of the table. She leaned down by him and examined his face, which was slowly regaining its color. "Are you all right?"

He used his hand to indicate he still didn't have his voice back.

"You're—you're sure?" he wheezed.

She straightened up. "Sure I'm pregnant or sure it's yours?"

He ignored her frosty tone. "Of course it's mine. I'm just asking if you'd seen a doctor for confirmation."

"I *am* a doctor."

"Yeah, for the average age range of what, six? Last I heard, pediatricians didn't get involved with a baby until it was out of the womb." By now, Brian's color had turned from purple to a startling shade of red. "When did you figure out you were pregnant?"

Now Gail's face was red. She mumbled something.

"What was that?" He cocked his ear. "I didn't quite hear you."

She pursed her lips. "I said that I didn't. My physician's assistant suggested I get tested after I'd been sick several mornings in a row."

"Oh yeah, Doc, nothing gets by you, does it?" Brian reached for his beer and downed a healthy gulp.

"I called you right after I left the doctor's office," she explained.

"And your reason being…?"

Gail had the chance to recover. "I wanted to assure you that you wouldn't have to worry about my asking for any financial assistance. Naturally, I have excellent health insurance and a small but nice stock portfolio."

"I am more than willing to contribute to the baby's welfare," he insisted.

"And I would like that, too."

Brian shook his head. He'd nursed one beer through

dinner, but now he was wondering if he'd missed something along the way.

Luckily, she didn't waste any time in putting him out of his misery.

"There are no financial worries, but I would like the baby to know his or her father. If that is all right with you," she said hesitantly. "You said you enjoyed children and wanted some of your own. Maybe not this soon." She blushed. "But since the baby is coming, I hope you'd be willing to be a part of his or her life. I'd like to see this kept as friendly as possible. What I mean is, I don't see why we would need to take this to court. I'd never deny you the chance to see your child."

"My brothers are never going to let me live this down," he muttered. He suddenly frowned as something occurred to him. "It just goes to show you can't afford to steal someone's condoms."

Gail nodded. "They say there can be failure at times."

"Wow, macho sperm." Brian chuckled. He caught her frown. "Sorry, I couldn't resist it." His grin kept growing until it seemed to split his face in two. "I'm going to be a dad. This is so—"

She looked at him, wary of what he'd say.

"Great."

She relaxed instantly. "I wasn't sure how you would take it. It's not as if this was planned," she said, fidgeting with her glass.

Brian's grin dimmed to a shadow of what it had been before. "What about you? How do you feel about this?" he asked, clearly inviting honesty. "As you said, this wasn't planned. Although, I guess if we used protection and you are on the pill and there's still a pregnancy, someone had plans for us we didn't know about."

Gail looked off into the distance. Her fingers didn't stray far from the glass so she had something to hang on to. She turned back to face Brian.

"Naturally, I was shocked at first. I thought I was either eating the wrong kinds of food or the flu hit me," she said softly. "I guess I hadn't thought about children as much as you had because I hadn't looked that far ahead. I knew I had enough to do in getting settled in my practice to think about anything more."

"And I guess you have major medical school loans to pay off, too," he said.

The blush started across her cheekbones and trailed up her temples.

"Actually, I don't," she admitted. "My parents were so happy I was going into what they considered a proper profession, they willingly covered all my expenses. They said then there was no excuse for me not to do well."

Brian thought of his siblings who'd worked more than one job to get through college, then usually helping the younger ones when it was their turn. Right now, he was helping Nikki with her tuition. He was suddenly grateful she wasn't planning on spending the next ten years in school.

"Something else we need to consider," he brought up. "The prospective grandparents. Have you told your parents yet?"

By now, he could tell when she wasn't comfortable with a subject. She'd look away as if she could find her answer in the distance. Even with the lights on around the patio, she somehow managed to stay shielded by the evening darkness.

"I was never all that sure they wanted me, so I have no idea how they'll feel about being grandparents." She shot him a wary look. "Do you think yours will be upset about this?"

"My mother will be happy there's one more baby to love. She thinks all her grandchildren were made just for her. She says she can spoil them rotten and feed them sugary snacks before sending them home to their parents who have to put up with the results." Brian looked at the puzzled look on Gail's face and came to a realization that stunned him. For a woman who made her living healing the young, she had no real idea about children in general. In a need to find out what he could about Gail, he'd been able to casually mention her to other paramedics and hospital staff. He learned she was highly liked and respected by both parents and patients alike. But nothing else. If she had a personal life, no one knew about it.

He saw a woman who'd been raised by indifferent parents, had no siblings and spent her childhood with little interaction with her peers. Yet, she still chose to treat children and apparently enjoyed doing so. He couldn't imagine a better mother for his child.

"Gail." He waited until she looked up at him. "We're going to be fine."

Then he waited for her to inform him she could do fine on her own, thank you very much.

But she surprised him by smiling wanly.

"Maybe we will at that."

GAIL HAD BEEN raised to be self-sufficient. Her parents had firmly believed there wasn't any situation that couldn't be worked out in a logical manner.

She remembered standing at the window watching other kids laughing and playing and her, inside her house either practicing the piano, which she hated, or reading Jane Austen, which she loved. Her parents never wanted her to play with the children. According to them, there was nothing she could learn from other children except bad habits. But even at a young age, she was convinced she could have learned a great deal from them.

She was glad her baby would have Brian for a father. She had no doubt her child would have the social advantages she wasn't allowed.

His joy in learning that he was going to be a father was sincere. Yet he had to have doubts. After all, he hardly knew her! Yet, he sat there and told her not to worry, that everything would be fine.

She should be upset her life had virtually been taken out of her hands. Changes made she hadn't planned for.

"Before I bought a refrigerator, I spent three months researching the top brands, deciding what features I wanted, which brands had fewer service problems, you name it," she said suddenly. "I did the same with all my major appliances." She seemed to laugh at herself. "Actually, I do that with small appliances, too. I've always planned everything well ahead. No surprises."

"Then you ask a stranger to be your date for a banquet, get carjacked, kidnapped, stranded, almost arrested and pregnant all in the space of twenty-four hours. I gotta tell you, Gail, when you blow your world to smithereens, you do it with style." He toasted her with his beer bottle.

Gail got to her feet and gathered up the plates. "My car was an innocent victim in all this," she muttered.

Brian quickly gathered up the rest of the plates and followed her inside. When she turned to face him, she bumped into him. She snatched the plates out of his hands.

"Why don't you go outside, and I'll bring out the pie," she told him.

"Why? So you can wrap yourself in that prickly exterior again?" he couldn't resist teasing. "Not allowed tonight." He hip-bumped her over to one side. "You sit down, and I'll get these dishes done in no time. Don't worry, I haven't broken anything in weeks."

Gail protested even as he settled her at the kitchen table. He even turned the chore of washing and drying into a game, which had her laughing at his stories about mealtime at the fire station.

For a brief second, she entertained the wild idea this was what it would be like if they were married. Not that she wanted to be a member of that institution. She'd decided a long time ago that marriage wasn't for her.

Of course, when she'd made that decision she hadn't thought all that much about motherhood. Now she faced it with a vengeance. Along with a man who made her feel things she didn't think she wanted to feel.

She attributed those feelings to her pregnancy and reminded herself that all that mattered was that he be there for their child. She could take care of herself just fine.

"I don't think tonight was ever covered in any book of manners," Brian said not long after. "So I'll just thank you for dinner and let you get your rest. Something you'll need more of now."

"So I've been told," she murmured, opening the front door.

If she expected him to just leave then, she forgot who she was dealing with. Brian settled his hands on her shoulders and leaned in for a kiss.

It was no light peck on the lips. He moved his mouth against hers in a slow leisurely manner that soon wasn't the least bit leisurely. He kicked the door shut again, swiveled around so she was pressed against the door and feasted on her mouth. By the time he lifted his head, they were both breathing hard.

"I'm not going to have sex with you," Gail said, even though her voice wasn't all that convincing to either of them. "Look what happened the last time we did!'

"Well, we wouldn't have to worry about it again, would we?" he joked then relented when he realized how serious she was. "It was just a kiss, Gail. Although it seems when we kiss, we have a lot of trouble stopping. Tonight was a big surprise for me. I know we have a lot of discussions ahead of us. Decisions to make. But I think we both need a good night's sleep first. How about I take you out for breakfast tomorrow?"

Gail grimaced. "I'm not usually my best in the morning."

"Okay, brunch then." He kissed her on the forehead. "I'll see you tomorrow. Lock the door after me. I'm not leaving until I hear the lock engaged."

She smiled as she made a production of throwing the dead bolt then setting the alarm.

"What on earth is that?" she asked herself when she heard a muted purr coming from out front. When she looked out the window, all she saw was a sportscar speeding down the road. "I wonder how that rattletrap truck of his snuck out of here without my hearing it?"

As she walked down the hallway to her bedroom, Gail was unaware she was caressing her abdomen protectively.

She'd done the right thing in telling Brian about the baby. He didn't blame her or become angry. He didn't resent her request or feel she was out to ruin his life.

She knew she had eight months to figure out how to handle the changes in her life. By then, she'd know how to schedule her life with the baby. How to schedule Brian into that life. And all would be fine.

BRIAN BARELY slept all night. He was going to be a father! In about eight months there would be a baby who would need him. He quickly changed his mind on that thought. The baby would probably appreciate his or her mother more in the beginning. Brian planned to be there when the baby was old enough to appreciate his or her dad.

Not once did he regret what happened. Not making love with Gail and not having a baby together. Maybe they didn't know each very well. But their bodies obviously recognized they were right for each other.

He knew he wasn't in love with Gail, but there was something between them he wanted to pursue. Now he had the chance to do it. He wondered if she would have called him if she hadn't ended up pregnant.

He'd be a good father. He knew he would. After all, he had the best dad in the world to learn from.

My little one, he thought to himself, warmed by the words.

THE EARTHQUAKE in her stomach registered at least an eight point nine.

Gail kept her eyes closed and focused on keeping her body as still as possible as the world rocked and rolled around her. Actually, it wasn't her world rolling but her stomach, but all she knew was that she dared not move a finger, blink her eyes or point her toes. Any, or all, could cause an upheaval she couldn't handle. She'd tried nibbling on a soda cracker, but that didn't stay down long.

"Go away," she whispered painfully when the musical chimes of her doorbell echoed throughout the house. A moment later, the chimes sounded again. "I'm not ready to face the public."

Brian. He'd told her he'd be by this morning. Little did she know she would be spending the time planning her funeral.

Gail's stomach continued roiling threats as she edged her way out of bed. She pulled on her robe and slowly made her way to the door.

"I was getting worried—" Brian stopped when he had a chance to get a good look at her. "Wow, you look really bad."

"Thank you so much for making my morning." She turned away and headed for the nice comfy couch in her family room. It was as good a place as any to die on. Brian stood uncertainly in the room. "So, I guess you don't feel like going out to breakfast."

"Go out to breakfast!" Her scratching response was halted by her throat convulsively working. She leaped off the couch and pushed him out of the way as she raced to the bathroom.

What could he do for her other than stand here like an idiot?

When she returned from the bathroom, her face was deathly pale and her movements listless.

"Here." He curved his arm around her waist and guided her over to the couch. She resisted, pointing, instead to a fat easy chair with a square hassock in front of it. Once she was settled, he grabbed the colorful afghan laid across the back and draped it over her lap. He got her a glass of water, found some crackers and brought them over.

"Do you have it this bad every morning?" he asked, sitting on the nearby hassock. When he realized her feet were bare, he picked them up and briskly rubbed them between his hands. "You should have taken the time to put on slippers," he chided.

"How did you know about the crackers?" she asked, nibbling on one.

"One sister who couldn't go anywhere without crackers in her purse, a sister-in-law who swore by them. Co-workers who talk about their wives' pregnancies. You can't help but pick up helpful hints." He laid her feet back down and covered them with the afghan. He looked at her with an unreadable gaze.

"You don't need to tell me," she said testily, clearly not liking his visual regard. "It's not just because I have no makeup on, hair flying in all directions and wearing a robe that's made for comfort and not looks. There's circles under my eyes, my skin is the color of library paste, and I look like something not even a cat would drag in. As you can imagine, I'm not in any mood for breakfast or anything else right now. So you can just run off and do whatever you do on your day off." She shifted under the afghan.

"Once those crackers stay down for you, we'll try a poached egg on toast," he suggested, easily ignoring her.

"Don't try that medical *we* on me," she snapped. "I can take care of myself." She started to raise up then suddenly thought better of it. She carefully placed her hand over her stomach obviously waiting for it to settle back down.

"Yeah, I can see that." Brian returned to the kitchen and made a thorough search of all the cabinets. It wasn't long before he had the soft egg nestled on a slice of toast. He cut it into bite-size pieces and brought it over to her. "Don't worry if you can't eat it all, but do what you can. Your stomach will feel better once you have something in it.'' He forked up a piece and held it before her lips.

Gail didn't say a word as she cautiously nibbled. When that seemed to help, she accepted a second. She'd eaten a little over half before she put the plate to one side.

"Not bad," he commented, whisking the plate out of sight. Just in case.

She took a deep breath. "Thank you for fixing me breakfast," she said reluctantly.

"You're eating for two now."

She rolled her eyes. "That is such a cliché."

"But true." He paused. "Unless…" He shot her a quick look. "Do multiple births run in your family?"

Gail gasped. "No! What about yours?"

He shook his head. "So we're safe there. Although my sister-in-law did have twins."

"The odds are in our favor," she corrected.

"I might not have minded twins or whatever, but I have an idea that you wouldn't feel as generous."

"True." She fiddled with the ends of the afghan. "Brian."

He waited for her to say more but all he heard for a few moments was silence. He finally gave up and was the first to break it.

"Yes?"

"I am grateful you fixed me breakfast, but I'm feeling better now. There's no reason for you to stay." This time when she sat up, she didn't turn pale. She swung her legs over the side and got to her feet. She picked up the afghan, carefully folded it, and arranged it over the back of the chair.

Brian remained seated on the couch. Now that he was here he wasn't ready to leave.

"Maybe there's something you need done around the house you can't do yourself."

"That's what I have Mr. Raymond for. He's my handyman who takes care of all those little chores that I can't do," she explained. "Just last week he fixed my patio screen door, replaced a broken lock on a window and replaced a washer in the kitchen sink."

"What? He didn't mow the lawn?"

"I have a gardening service." She arched an eyebrow.

"Go ahead and shower and dress and whatever else you need to do," he urged. "You'll feel better after you do."

She pushed away hair that hung lankly around her face. "Thank you so much for again pointing out how horrible I look. Thank you again for breakfast. Now, please go."

"No, that's not it!" He knew it was time to backpedal. He just wasn't sure how far back to go. "Look, I'm not doing this very well."

"No kidding."

Brian ignored her droll tone. "At least let me do the dishes first. It's only fair since I cooked. And one less thing for you to worry about." He gently pushed her out of the room. "Go take your shower. I'll clean up, and then we'll decide what to do with the rest of the day."

"I already have plans for the day," she muttered, heading for her bedroom. Why bother arguing any longer when a shower was exactly what she wanted.

Once he heard the water running, Brian decided to do some sleuthing. He rationalized his snooping with the explanation it would give him a better idea about the prospective mother of his child.

A bag of French vanilla decaf coffee beans was lined up in front of a bag of caffeinated coffee beans. Spices were arranged alphabetically, although he couldn't see anything special in the meager assortment. Obviously, she didn't do a lot of cooking. No cookbooks, no stash of ice cream in the freezer, cookies or candy in the cupboards.

"She sure eats damn healthy, even for a doctor," he muttered, closing the last cabinet door. "Didn't she ever learn that chocolate is the fifth food group?"

"Funny, I wasn't aware there was a fifth food group." Gail, now showered and dressed, stood in the kitchen doorway.

Brian wasn't the least bit embarrassed being caught snooping. "You ask my sisters and they'll tell you there is. Once a month, when they turn into raving maniacs, it's best if there's chocolate in the house. My brother would prefer to arrange his duty time around my sister-in-law's schedule." He narrowed his eyes at her. "Does this really happen to every woman on the planet where a guy feels he has to duck and cover?"

She smiled so sweetly, he was convinced cotton candy was the cause. "You men really need to lighten up. Years ago, when women physicians were having their periods they weren't allowed in the operating room. It was thought they would suddenly turn insane and butcher their patients."

Brian couldn't hold back his laughter. He had to lean against the counter so he wouldn't fall to the floor. When he finally realized that Gail wasn't sharing his merriment, his laughter stopped and started a few times until it died down.

"Not a joke?"

She slowly shook her head. "Very much not a joke. I've heard some of the old school doctors still believe that old wives' tale. Women doctors still aren't taken seriously in some specialties."

Brian shook his head. Not in surprise but in understanding. He might not have a medical degree, but he had years of training and what he knew, he knew well. No matter what some doctors might say.

He looked her up and down. He guessed her blue knit polo shirt, pressed no less, khaki pants with a sharp crease and brown loafers were perfect for work, but not on a weekend when a person is supposed to have fun!

"Don't you own a pair of jeans?" he asked.

Gail looked puzzled. "Why would I wear jeans?"

"Because it's Saturday, and on Saturdays, when people don't work, they wear jeans or shorts or at least something casual," he explained patiently. "Something they don't care about getting dirty when they're working in the yard or around the house." He heaved a sigh. "Come on, Doc. We need to get you outside in the fresh air." He walked over and grabbed her hand.

"I can't just go out!" Gail panicking, tried to hold back, but he was having none of it.

"Why not?"

"I have things to do!"

"Like what?"

She racked her brain but couldn't come up with an excuse that sounded plausible. She had to run to keep up with Brian's long strides as he hauled Gail out of the house.

"Brian! I'm not some piece of luggage you can drag around," she protested, unsuccessfully trying to tug her hand free.

"You'll have fun, you'll see," he promised, snagging her purse along the way and handing it to her.

Gail's next protest stilled on her lips when she saw where they were headed. Dominating her driveway was a snazzy-looking blue-and-white Corvette convertible with the top down. She knew next to nothing about cars, but she did know this car was more than thirty years old and considered very valuable.

"This is yours?"

Brian opened the passenger door with a flourish. "All mine." He ushered her into the leather bucket seat and closed the door after her.

"But the truck—?" She turned in the seat as he settled himself behind the wheel.

"The truck's my dad's pride and joy. It may look like a junk heap, but it's got an engine under the hood that could make a man weep. This is more me." He slid a pair of aviator-style sunglasses off the visor and slipped them on. "Although, I guess a baby seat wouldn't exactly fit in here."

Gail privately agreed with his assessment. She still wasn't sure why she allowed him to kidnap her, even if she didn't think she had a choice. Brian seemed to prefer to sweep a person along like a hurricane. Not her idea of fun.

If she thought about it, she couldn't say just what was her idea of fun. It didn't seem to matter since Brian was going to show her his.

Chapter Seven

"I can't do this!"

"Sure you can. You did it as a kid, didn't you?" he told her in a mellow voice meant to assuage her fears. Except they didn't.

Gail lowered her voice so only Brian could hear her. "People are staring, Brian. And no, I didn't do it as a child."

"No one's staring." He didn't even bother looking around to see if what she said was true. He knew she was doing her best out of doing what he knew was best for her. He kept hold of her hands as she struggled for her balance.

She looked like a cornered puppy. "I'll fall down," she warned in a harsh whisper. "A pregnant woman should not fall down."

He grinned. "Nice try, Doc." He briefly placed his hand against her abdomen. There wasn't even the barest of curves there yet. "But the kid here is about as safe as he or she can be. There's no way I'd let you do anything that could be considered unsafe. Not to mention you're wearing padding for the areas that tend to get hurt if you fall. Just hang on to me, and you'll be fine."

She did just that as she felt her feet start to give out from under her.

"I couldn't roller-skate, so what makes you think I can in-line skate," she gasped, grabbing his arm for balance.

"Because this will be easier. Just remember to glide from the side, not the front," he instructed as he started them off on a slow pace. "Relax, Gail."

Her breaths came in short harsh puffs as she concentrated on his instructions along with keeping her feet on the ground, so to speak. She realized by keeping her gaze firmly planted on the ground that she felt a bit more in control.

"Look around you, Gail," he coaxed, still keeping a firm hold on her hands as he skated around to skate backward so he could face her. "You're doing fine. If you'd just relax you might even start to enjoy yourself."

She didn't venture a smile as if even that small gesture would cause her to lose her balance. The wide park trail was set aside for walkers and skaters. It seemed by unspoken agreement, the trail was mostly used by the walkers early in the morning and early evening while those with in-line skates frequented it during late mornings and the afternoons.

Luckily, there were only a few souls out that day even if Gail felt they were multiplied hundred-fold every time she dared to look around. She would have bet everything she owned that there were squirrels in the trees laughing at her.

"Come on, Gail." His whisper wafted warm against her ear. "If you'd let yourself go a little, you'd find it a hell of a lot more fun."

"Maybe this isn't my idea of fun." She felt her legs start to wobble and she tightened her hold on him.

"Exercise is good during pregnancy."

She tried to stop but discovered all her efforts did was almost send both of them sprawling to the ground. Only Brian's quick reflexes kept them from disaster.

"Do not tell me what is good during pregnancy," she enunciated each word with deadly accuracy. "I know what is good during pregnancy."

"You know what you learned during an OB rotation, but that doesn't tell you everything. I heard all you learn is how to catch a baby or how to perform a flawless C-section." Brian urged her to continue skating.

Gail would have preferred to chew nails than admit that was pretty much what her rotation was like. It hadn't taken her long to discover that she preferred spending time with the tiny newborns than with the new mothers.

"All pregnancies are not run-of-the-mill. We always had to be alert for anything out of the ordinary," she informed him with a haughty air.

Brian spoiled her lady-of-the-manor attitude with a hearty laugh. "Sure you did. And immediately hand the case over to the patient's doctor because you weren't trusted to handle anything too important."

"Not all doctors are like that," she argued. She was soon so caught up in their verbal exchange she started to forget what her feet were doing.

"No, not all of them are, but I've seen both kinds. They're everywhere, Doc. Just like fleas." He gradually released one hand and lightened his hold on the other until only their fingers touched.

"You can't lump them all under one general term," Gail continued debating, now unaware she was skating alone. "It's that way in every profession and you know it. I'm sure there are paramedics out there who feel the new ones don't know a thing and are good for nothing more than driving the vehicle. Am I right or not?'' Not receiving an immediate answer, she looked around. And found Brian grinning a couple of feet behind her. *"Wha—!''* She flailed her arms but didn't fall because Brian caught her in time.

She took several deep breaths to calm her erratic pulse.

"Do not ever do that again," she ordered.

"You didn't even notice," he jeered, grinning broadly at her.

Gail didn't think twice. Before Brian could realize what was happening, her fist was planted in his stomach. He let out an *"Oof!''* of air. With him cradling his tender stomach and her action putting her off balance, she had no one to grab as she felt herself start to fall backward. Brian muttered a curse and reached out for her, but it was too late. Gail found herself landing so painfully on her rear end even her teeth felt jarred.

Feeling stunned, she sat there with her legs sprawled out in front of her. When she shifted her gaze upward, it was to find Brian holding his hand out to her.

"I guess you had to prove your point by falling where you're not as well padded."

Gail took hold of his hand but instead of allowing him to pull her up, she yanked backward with all her strength. She felt great satisfaction when he fell forward just narrowly missing landing on his nose.

"I gather you had the same problem," she said with saccharine sweetness. How upset her family would be with her for acting like a regular hoyden. Gail didn't care because her retaliation felt way too good.

Brian rolled over onto his side, propping his head up with his hand.

"You are a nasty woman," he told her, making his way to his feet and pulling her up before she could think up any more mischief. He guided them over to the side of the path and a wooden bench.

Gail winced as her abused rear end touched the hard surface.

Brian bent forward and unlaced his skates. He pulled on his running shoes, which had been draped around his neck with the laces tied together. He'd slipped Gail's loafers into his jeans pockets. He took care of her skates next.

"Now you look better," he told her.

"Of course, my hair is a mess. My hands are scraped, and I feel sore all over," she grumbled.

"Maybe so, but there's color in your face, and I'd say you're feeling more lively than you did when I first saw you this morning. You needed fresh air and—"

"If you say the word *exercise* one more time..." she warned, leaning toward him.

He held his hands up in surrender. "Are you kidding? After that last stunt, I'm not doing that again."

Gail looked around. The woodsy park was new to her although it turned out not to be all that far from her house. Somewhat hilly, it sported many hiking trails and a large playground, which she visualized coming back to when the baby was old enough to enjoy it.

She thought of all she'd planned to do today. She had dry cleaning to pick up, grocery shopping to do, pick up a few things at the drugstore, and numerous other errands that only she would consider important. So why was she sitting here breathing in air redolent with flowers? Not thinking beyond getting up and maybe even trying again.

Maybe it had something to do with the company.

With Brian sitting so close to her, she could detect a scent coming from his warm male skin. That hint of spice again. He had tipped his baseball cap over his eyes and leaned back with his legs stretched out in front of him, crossed at the ankles. He was the poster boy for pure relaxation.

"Is this what you do on your day off?" she asked.

Brian opened one eye. "This or something else. It's a crime to stay indoors when it's nice like this. You need to be out and enjoying it. Something I don't think you do all that often."

Gail squirmed under his perception. "I'm outside a lot," she defended herself. "But I also have obligations. I don't have a lot of free time to just indulge myself."

His grin brought a flutter to the pit of her stomach. When she thought about it, she got that flutter every time he grinned.

"Indulging yourself is good for the soul, Doc," he rumbled. "If you're going to have a kid, you need to learn to play like a kid."

"My parents didn't 'play like a kid' and they did very well."

He shrugged. "Music lessons, classical concerts, afternoons in museums and art galleries. Ballet lessons. Oh yeah, a well-rounded upbringing."

Gail looked away. Again, Brian had pretty much hit the nail on the head. Any free time she had was spent just that way. Her parents wanted her well-versed in the arts so she could be productive as the perfect wife for a company executive her father would have chosen for her if she'd allowed him. The only time she broke free of the mold they'd set for her was when she chose to go into medicine. She was surprised when her father took care of her tuition. Until he explained it would be one less worry for her as she pursued a suitable career. And hopefully found a suitable husband while she was at it. The day he said that was the day she set up a special savings account. She planned to pay her father back every penny he spent on her medical school education.

"Children who don't have some structure in their lives only end up getting into trouble," she told him, unthinkingly parroting words her own father had used more than once.

"Children can have structure in their lives and still have fun, Gail." Brian stood up and turned around, grabbing her hands and pulling her to her feet. "Come on. I'm ready for lunch, and I'm sure you are, too."

She took a mental tally and nodded. "But I want to go home after we eat. No matter what, I still have errands to run."

Brian looked down at Gail and noticed the color in her face from their skating. He was positive she'd be horrified when she discovered there were grass stains on her rumpled shirt and pants. Her braid was coming undone, and her lipstick had disappeared long ago.

She still tried to come across as the well-groomed woman, but now he wouldn't buy it. She did look good mussed up a little.

Now all he had to do was convince her of that fact.

IT DIDN'T TAKE Brian long to discover Gail's secret vice. All it took was a restaurant that offered old-fashioned milk shakes. Once she saw them featured on the menu, her eyes lit up. She didn't waste any time in ordering a chocolate shake.

"No saying you just want a salad," he warned.

He was positive his heart slammed against his chest when she smiled. Gail Roberts with a free-for-all smile like this was enough to blow his mind. He hadn't seen her often, but when he did she rarely smiled as if life itself was very serious business. Maybe that was why he wanted to show her that life could be pretty fun. If you had the right person showing you that fun.

"I don't think you need to worry there," she assured him. "Mornings may be bad, but I make up for it later on." She looked up at the waitress. "I'd like a cheeseburger, everything on it but onions and your seasoned curly fries. And another shake, please."

"I'll have the same, but a large Coke instead of the shake," Brian told her.

After the waitress left, he watched Gail. Did she know how approachable she looked now with her hair still slightly mussed and clothing less than impeccable? He bet she looked fantastic in a pair of jeans.

In another time, he wouldn't have given her a second glance. She was too well put together for him. He liked his women a bit mussed. Ready for adventure at a moment's notice.

He'd hazard a good guess that Gail's idea of adventure was going on her errands in the order she had them listed on a piece of paper.

Maybe he could change that.

Gail bit into her cheeseburger with a hunger she'd been trying to tamp down until the food arrived. All it took was the hearty aroma of charbroiled meat and melted cheese to send her drooling in anticipation. She'd eaten half her burger before she started to slow down and enjoy the food. She picked up a fry, daintily dipped it in ketchup and nibbled on it.

"This is very good."

"Glad to hear it." Watching the way she was demolishing her food, he figured he'd have to do some fast eating to keep up with her.

"That wasn't so bad, was it?" Brian asked as they later sped down the street.

Gail hesitated, then smiled and shook her head. "Fine, I'll say just what you want to hear. You were right. It was nice to get out in the fresh air."

"It's the best thing for you. It clears the head and revs up the energy level." He grinned.

"And hurts the butt," she muttered, moving a bit stiffly now. "I should have asked you what you had in mind. I wasn't very good at roller-skating as a child."

"You did great, so don't sell yourself short." Brian looked down at her appreciating the windblown appearance she now sported. Yep, maybe there was hope for her yet.

He was tempted to kiss her. Right now, she looked damn kissable.

"I guess we didn't get all that much talking done," he said in a low voice as he helped her out of the car.

She offered a small smile as they walked up to her door. "No, you decided to sweep me off to the park for some unbearable torture. I guess I should be grateful you fed me afterward."

"Yeah, I usually don't feed women I've tortured," he quipped, waiting as she unlocked her door and disarmed the security alarm. He touched her arm to stop her from walking farther into her house. "I better go so you can do all those errands you need to do." He slid his hand down her arm and laced his fingers through hers. He gave it a gentle tug to bring her closer to him. "No more avoiding my calls?"

She blushed as she realized he knew what she'd been doing. "I'll take your calls as long as you realize there are no ties here." She looked him in the eye as she said that so he'd know how serious she was.

He looked her back square in the eye even though he was about as committed as he could be.

"Just don't ask me to change diapers," he joked, determined to keep it light.

"We'll discuss that later on." She smiled. She reached up, kissed him on the cheek, and disappeared into the house.

Brian whistled under his breath as he walked back to his car. Yep, things were looking up.

GAIL FINISHED her errands in record time. Other weekends she hadn't thought about how quiet her off time was. Groceries picked up and put away. Laundry was taken care of in record time. Dry cleaning taken off the wire hangers and put on padded ones. Checkbook balanced to the penny.

She should have been satisfied with herself. Instead, she wandered around the house, stopping at one of the guest rooms and trying to visualize it as a nursery. Streams of blue and pink seemed to swirl in front of her eyes, and she grabbed hold of the doorway to keep her balance. She could feel panic starting to take over.

Gail didn't waste any time in making her way to the family room where she collapsed on her comfy easy chair and propped her feet up on the matching hassock. She dragged the afghan over her body. She suddenly felt very cold even though it was warm in the room.

She thought of the life growing inside her and the panic only intensified.

"I can't do this," she whispered, pulling the afghan up to her chin as if it would shield her from the world.

''My parents didn't know how to be parents. How can I know what to do?

''There has to be a mistake somewhere because I am very definitely not mother material.''

Chapter Eight

"Well?" Sheila pounced on Gail the moment she walked through the office's back door.

"Good morning to you, too." Gail stopped by the reception desk to pick up her messages before heading for her office.

"You have a full day," Lora warned her.

Gail thought about her tummy that had behaved so far that morning. She only hoped it would continue to do so. She'd spent most of the previous day in bed with soda crackers and flat 7Up by her bed. It wasn't until evening that she started to feel more like herself.

She was going to have to tell her office mates soon. With everyone in the area it seemed as good a time as any.

"Everyone," she said hesitantly. Public speaking had never been one of her strengths. Starting now wasn't what she'd planned. "I have something to say."

Ted Chang, one of the other pediatricians in the office, grinned. "Considering you never make announcements, this one must be a real doozy."

Moira pointedly glanced at her watch. "I do hope this won't take long," she drawled. "I have a patient due any time."

For a moment, Gail lost her nerve. For a woman who was known for her cool self-composure, she couldn't find it now.

"I—ah—" *How to put this* "I just wanted to say that I may have to lighten my load in the next few months since I'm pregnant." *There, to the point and concise.*

"I knew it!" Sheila screamed, jumping up and down. "I knew it!"

"Don't worry about the shell shock, kid." Ted may have only been three years older than she, but he enjoyed lording those thirty-six months over her. "It will wear off as your tummy grows. Cyn will tell you that."

Gail thought of Ted's wife who seemed to regard pregnancy as a game and never lost her figure. Along with juggling four children she handled a thriving legal practice, and no one seemed to lack for attention. Gail thought of her as a woman who truly had it all and did it all well.

"No wonder you've been barfing so much," Sheila spun her in a circle. She abruptly stopped. "Oops, as one who's survived those wars, I should have remembered that any sudden turns aren't good."

Gail held tightly on to her hands as her stomach took a couple of nosedives. Luckily, they subsided. "Yes."

"So the father's the one who sent you the flowers?" Lora asked excitedly.

Moira's smile wasn't all that friendly as she passed by Gail. "I guess they're right after all about those still waters," she murmured before heading back to her office.

Gail could only release a huge sigh of relief. "I thought about it over the weekend and knew I'd have to say something sooner or later. I decided to just get it over with."

Doug came up and gave her a hug and kiss. "Anything you need, you know where to come," he said.

"What about the father?" Sheila asked with her usual forthright attitude.

"Not now," she said under her breath, walking toward her office as quickly as possible. "I have a full day, remember?"

As if an afterthought, Gail made a swift detour toward the ladies' room.

Sheila looked after her with feminine sympathy.

"Something tells me you're going to spend a lot of time in there."

THE MOMENT Brian stepped inside the station he sensed something was up. For one thing, it was much too quiet.

Which could only mean one thing.

He stepped into the room that was combination kitchen, dining area and television room. He barely had one foot in before a raucous rendition of "Rockabye Baby" sounded with his brother leading the off-key chorus. He shook his head and dropped into a chair someone thoughtfully provided.

Blue and pink balloons floated along the ceiling while the center of the table boasted a large cake with a plastic baby carriage decorating the center. Wildly wrapped packages circled the cake.

"My big brother is going to be a dad, guys," Mark loudly announced, brushing away an imaginary tear.

Brian looked at the decorations. A plastic baby smoking a cigar instead of holding a baby bottle had him shuddering while another baby wearing a fireman's hat had him shaking his head.

"You shouldn't have, guys. You really shouldn't have." He hoped he could inject as much sincerity into that comment as he could. Because from past experience, when he'd planned such parties, he knew this was only the beginning.

"It's the least we can do for one of our own," Rick, Brian's fellow paramedic, told him. "When Mark and Jeff gave us the news, we wanted to do something special for you. Especially after all the parties you've planned for us in the past."

Brian winced. He feared Rick was thinking of the condom and vitamin E decorated tree Brian gave him at his bachelor party. He looked up at the balloon-covered ceiling. Luckily, they were real balloons.

"So, Mark, I guess your job was blowing up all those balloons since you're the only one with enough hot air." He got up and took a closer look at the cake. Like Gilligan, Three Hours Turned into More than Expected was written in blue frosting.

"Here you go, Dad," Brad, one of the firemen sliced a piece of cake and handed it to Brian. "So, when do we get to meet the little mother?"

"Not in this lifetime." Yum, lemon filling. His favorite.

"The women aren't going to let you get away with that," Rick warned him. "You know how it works around here. Here, open your gifts." He tossed him a wrapped package.

Brian stared at the wrapping that was more X-rated than G-rated. "Gee, thanks, Sinclair."

"How'd he know?" Walt Sinclair looked around at the others.

"Who else uses wrapping paper that can't be bought unless you're over the age of twenty-one!" someone ribbed.

Brian had to admit each gift was thoughtfully chosen.

He held up a set of earplugs.

"You wear those so she's the one getting up when the baby cries."

He couldn't believe the next. "Nose plugs?"

"Dirty diapers!"

The last gift turned out to be a toy model of a minivan.

"No room for a baby seat in your baby," Mark said. "So, who gets the 'Vette now that you'll be looking for something with a roomy back seat?"

"No one." Brian scowled at his brother.

"What did Cathy and Lou say about the impending grandchild?" someone asked.

"I haven't had a chance to tell them yet," he muttered. "They took the train up to Seattle and won't be back until later this week."

All the men exchanged looks. With the men working together so much and risking their lives together, they were a close-knit group. Brian's parents were a part of it as they opened their large home to the men any time there was a gathering going on. Cathy and Lou Walker treated all the men and their families as their own, and the feelings were returned.

"Which means you haven't gotten the lecture from Lou yet," one muttered.

Not something Brian wanted to think about, either.

"Look, Gail's a great lady," he said. "And if you morons ever do meet her I want you to treat her as such."

"Hey, we have manners," Brad said, offended Brian would think otherwise.

"So do apes, but they're not always good."

Any more retorts were halted by the sound of the bell

and a disembodied voice announcing a vehicle accident on the freeway.

The men wasted no time in racing for their vehicles.

"Knowing you, this is all going to work out," Rick said, clapping his friend on the back as they climbed into their paramedic truck. "You've always wanted kids and that's a plus right there. Think if you didn't. A lot of guys would be feeling pretty down now. You'll do good."

"Yeah, I will. Once I get all the answers."

"I CAN'T BELIEVE you just said that."

"Why not? It's true."

"But I don't want that!"

"No offense, but what about what *I* want here. I thought I had some say in this."

Gail pressed her fingers to her temples with the hope she could rub her headache away, but it didn't seem to be working.

When Lora told her Brian was on the phone, she thought he was calling to ask how she was. Yes, he did that, but he also asked when her next doctor's appointment was and announced he wanted to go with her.

"Gail, it took two people to make this baby, and there should be two people with the baby from the beginning," he said quietly.

"I told you, you didn't have to worry about my thinking you'll marry me because of the baby."

"That's not what I'm talking about and you know it."

She hated him for saying he wouldn't marry her because of the baby. Maybe she wasn't looking for marriage, but did he have to put it into words? Didn't an honorable man offer marriage when the woman ended up pregnant?

She hated herself because her pants didn't fit, her skirts were too snug and she was positive her tummy was pouching out. The only pants she could wear today were dry clean only rayon that she would never wear to work. Which was why her first patient, nine-year-old Sam Turner threw up all over her. Poor Gail didn't have a chance as she, in turn, threw up on Sam's brand-new tennis shoes with flashing lights around the soles.

Luckily, Sheila had a pair of knit pants stashed away. They were a little too long and snug in the waist but they would do while Gail's pants were utilizing one-hour service at the dry cleaners.

A nasty pinch under her arm was a reminder she needed to purchase some bras in a larger size along with pants and skirts with an elastic waistband. She nibbled on a soda cracker.

"Still having morning sickness?" Brian asked.

"I don't know why they call it morning sickness when you can have it any time day or night," she grumbled. "How did you know I wasn't feeling well?"

"I can hear the crunch of the crackers you're eating."

She muttered less than complimentary words about men with excellent hearing.

"When's your appointment?"

"You don't need to go with me." Her mother would have been horrified to hear her arguing. Gail never argued. It wasn't done. Suggesting one's point of view was an entirely different story and perfectly acceptable.

"Yes, I do. I'm the *father*." He stressed the last word.

She winced. "Fine, it's Thursday at three. Too bad if you're on duty because I'm not changing the appointment."

"Actually, I'm not. Since I'm sure you'll be working until then, I'll pick you up at the office."

"You don't need to do that," she protested.

"No prob, my sweet. I'll be there at two." He hung up before she could say anything.

Gail closed her eyes and rubbed her aching temples with her fingertips again. "I hope I'm having a girl. Another Brian Walker in this world just would not be a good idea."

GAIL TOLD HERSELF that she wouldn't allow Brian to take over. After all, it was still her life. She'd been saying that every day as if saying it kept him away. Except he was due here at any moment to drive her to the doctor's office.

When her phone buzzed, she already knew what she would hear.

"Doctor Roberts, Mr. Walker is here," Lora said in her best officious voice.

"Thank you, Lora. Send him on back."

The minute she heard Brian's deep tones mixed with Sheila's lighter ones, she realized her mistake.

"Believe me, we're keeping a close eye on her," she could hear Sheila say. "She needs to talk to the doctor about all that nausea she's still having. By now, mine was all gone."

"She'll tell him," Brian assured her.

She will tell the doctor what is necessary and nothing more. Gail flung open the door. She speared Sheila with a dark gaze. "Don't you have something to do?"

"I am," she said brightly. "I'm escorting Brian to your office."

"I'm sure Lora told him where it was."

"I didn't want him to get lost." Sheila smiled winningly at Brian who smiled back at her. His smile grew broader when he turned to Gail.

"Hi."

"Hi," she said, for lack of anything else.

The woman who was known for her cool composure. Known for her unflappable attitude where nothing unnerved her. Yet all she had to do was look at this man and she'd suddenly forget her own name. How could one pair of blue eyes and an engaging grin do this to her?

But he did have such incredible eyes. And she enjoyed looking at his eyes. And the rest of him.

Today, he wore a pair of navy pants and a white cotton shirt with the sleeves partially rolled up to reveal deeply tanned forearms. A thin pale line along the back of his neck showed signs of a recent haircut and he looked too good to be true.

To get her mind off how good he looked, she turned away to pick up her purse.

"Let's go." Her keys jingled as she dug them out of her bag. Her gaze was challenging. "Any problem with my driving?"

"Not as long as we take the freeway." He grinned, ignoring the explosive glare she flashed him.

"It's nice meeting you, Brian," Sheila sang out behind them as they headed for the rear exit.

"You too, Sheila. Thanks," he called over his shoulder as he ambled off behind Gail's swiftly retreating figure.

"What are you thanking her for?" she asked in a suspicion laden tone.

"For keeping an eye out on you."

Gail should have hated him for being truthful. She silently vowed to later discuss that fact with Sheila.

"You're looking good," Brian told Gail as she stopped by a dark-colored four-door sedan.

"Only because my breakfast and lunch stayed down today." She depressed the power lock button on her key ring.

"Decided against another convertible?" He settled in and secured the seat belt after adjusting the seat to accommodate his long legs.

"Considering everything, it's a good thing I didn't get another one." As she sat down she detected the faint scent of Brian's aftershave blending with the scent of her perfume already marking the car as her vehicle.

"My parents are having a barbecue this weekend. I was wondering if you'd like to come," Brian said, once Gail got on the road.

Her hands slid across the steering wheel.

"They want to take a look at me? See if I'm suitable?"

"They've been out of town so they don't even know about you yet," he said patiently. "The whole family turns up at these things. I thought you might want to see what great kids we Walker men make."

"Nothing major about your ego, is there?" she muttered.

"Not where it counts." He grinned, not the least bit offended. "All my brothers are the same way. You'll find out on Saturday."

"I didn't say I'd go," Gail reminded him.

"No, but you will. You need to relax and have fun, remember? I bet you didn't do anything the least bit fun last weekend, did you?"

She thought of the errands she'd accomplished, medical journals she perused and how she'd cleaned out her home office files, so anything she needed would be at her fingertips.

"I accomplished a great deal," she said primly.

Brian shook his head in mock consternation. "Oh, Doc, and here I thought I'd taught you better. Days off are to be enjoyed, remember?"

She shot him a quick glance as she slowed for a yellow light. "There's such a thing as grown-up responsibilities."

"Yes, there are. And there's also times when a grown-up needs to remember what it's like to be a kid. Best thing to know when you're raising kids."

Gail smiled. Now she could easily turn the tables on him. "Then I imagine you never got away with a thing when you were a boy."

"True," he freely admitted. "None of us were able to get away with skipping school because our dad seemed to know not only if one of us did but who it was. Mom was just as good with our sisters. We never had a chance. I guess with so many kids, they needed more than a few tricks up their sleeves to keep us in line. As Mom now says, none of us ended up in jail, so they must have done something right."

Gail's mind whirled. She worried about one child and Brian's parents worried about five. She felt more inadequate by the minute. She was never so relieved as when they arrived at the doctor's office.

She parked her car and waited a moment after she shut off the engine.

"This is still *my* doctor's appointment. Not yours," she said quietly. "Which means you will be seen but not heard."

He sat there quietly. "Can I go in with you when you see the doctor?"

She stared straight ahead. "No."

"Can I ask questions?"

"No."

He considered her replies. "So I'm basically along because I wanted to be here, and you figured it would be easier to let me come along than not. But that's it. I'm just here as a warm body."

Unbidden the memory of Brian's *very hot* body nestled against hers flashed across her senses. Her lower body started tingling and humming at the graphic memories. His hands creating magic on her skin while his mouth feasted on her as if she were a sumptuous banquet. Blaming it on hormones, she mentally shook herself back to the present.

"Have to go in," she murmured, unbuckling her seat belt.

Brian couldn't remember seeing so many pregnant women in one place. Then he reminded himself he was in an obstetrician's office.

"You must be due pretty soon," he commented to a twentyish woman who looked as if a watermelon would soon burst from her.

She gave him the wry look most overly pregnant women give a man who makes such an obvious comment.

"Very good." She could have been complimenting her dog for shaking hands. "How long have you been psychic?"

"I'm a paramedic and after a while, you can judge a due date pretty good," he explained. "Not your first, is it?"

"Third and last," she informed him. "I told my husband if he wants a fourth, he has to carry it himself."

"What are you doing?" Gail whispered, grabbing at his arm.

"Making conversation and being friendly," he replied in a low voice. "One thing I've always noticed about pregnant women is that they like to talk, and they love to share what they're going through.''

Gail overheard just enough of a conversation focusing on episiotomies and felt it best to tune out anything further. She was quickly learning that just because she was a doctor, it didn't mean it made it easier. All it did was take the mystery out of childbirth.

''Gail Roberts,'' a nurse called out.

Gail took a deep breath and stood up. Brian started to stand up but she pushed him back down.

''You may have seen me naked, but you won't be seeing me examined,'' she whispered fiercely.

''I want to at least meet the doctor.'' He put on his best stubborn expression. Judging by the resigned expression on her face, she knew she wouldn't win this battle.

''I'll have you called in when the examination is over,'' she said between clenched teeth before stalking off.

The woman on the other side of him reached over and patted his hand. ''Hormones are hell on us,'' she said. ''Makes us crazy at times. I'm afraid it's something you just have to contend with.''

''I'm learning.''

Brian contented himself with scanning magazines and checking his watch. His few visits to the doctor were mainly to update his allergy medication or the time he suffered a bad case of the flu. Brothers and friends talked about accompanying their wives to the obstetrician. Now he realized they hadn't parted with any helpful hints.

''Mr. Walker?'' A woman wearing a lab coat looked toward him.

He sprang to his feet, almost tripping over them. A

few women tittered. He grinned and sketched an elaborate bow.

"Dr. Riggs and Dr. Roberts are waiting for you in Dr. Riggs's office," she explained leading him down the hallway.

He heard the sound of shared laughter before anything else. The nurse knocked softly on the door before opening it.

Brian walked in and stopped short. Gail, looking more happy and relaxed than Brian had seen her, sat on a couch talking to a man seated next to her. The man looked up and smiled.

"You must be Brian. Come in and sit down," he invited.

Brian sat down but still couldn't stop staring.

"Did anyone ever tell you that you—?"

"All the time," Dr. Riggs chuckled. "I guess that's why my waiting room is so crowded all the time."

Any questions Brian had flew right out of his mind. The only thing he knew was that he didn't want this man seeing Gail naked!

"YOU WERE the one who wanted to meet the doctor then you sat there like a lump," Gail grumbled, when they returned to her car.

"Maybe it has something to do with your having a doctor who could be Mel Gibson's twin brother." He was still reeling. "Why didn't you tell me?"

"There was no reason to tell you. I went through medical school with John, and I never thought about his looks."

"No wonder every woman in there had on full makeup and looked dressed to kill," he muttered. He suddenly twisted in his seat and stared at Gail. "And you let him examine you!"

"Funny thing about doctors. That's what they do," she said calmly, pulling out of the parking lot. "How else can they know how you're doing if they don't examine you."

"Yeah, but my doctor doesn't examine my..." he stopped.

"Last I remember, you don't have one," she said sweetly. "Are you hungry? I'm starving."

"You're changing the subject."

"You know what sounds good? Shrimp. Lots of it. I don't eat deep-fried foods all that much, but right now shrimp sounds very good." She glanced around. "There's a good seafood restaurant not far from here. How does that sound to you?"

"Fine." He knew he sounded grumpy, but he didn't care.

If Brian had looked at Gail just then he would have seen a tiny smile on her lips that in any other woman he would have found fascinating. In Gail Roberts, it could only be considered dangerous.

Chapter Nine

Brian, who could usually eat any time, anywhere wasn't ready for food when they entered the restaurant. Nor was he in the best of the moods. He could see Gail was. And he had an idea it had something to do with him.

He was jealous of her doctor! Jealous, hell. He was downright crazy.

Her doctor looked like a film star. Had a personality that probably turned any woman to mush, and his job involved looking at naked women all day.

Okay, he didn't look at them the way a man looked at a naked woman in a magazine or on the screen. Or even when the mood involved wine and candlelight. As a member of the medical field, Brian knew that.

It didn't make him feel any better.

"Would either of you like a drink?" A scantily clad waitress stopped by their table.

"Club soda with a twist of lime," Gail requested.

"Beer. Whatever you have on tap is fine," Brian said.

He looked around, noticed how quiet the restaurant was due to the early hour. Even the bar hadn't filled up for Happy Hour yet.

"It seems you do know how to have fun. It's just that

you prefer mental instead of physical," he grumbled once he'd gotten his beer and taken a few sips.

"You were the one who insisted on going with me." She broke off a piece of the warm sourdough bread round loaf and lightly buttered it.

"You still want it your way." He didn't accuse her, just stated a fact.

"Yes."

Brian inclined his head in acknowledgement that she didn't back down or try to twist his words. He had to admit she was honest. And stubborn. But then, so was he. He watched her nibble on her bread. He had a desire to take her off somewhere so she could nibble on him.

Not that this feeling was anything new. He was used to spending his nights dreaming about Gail. More than once he questioned himself about the way he felt about her the first time he met her. How he saw her as the complete opposite of himself and very definitely not his type. Then there was the night they spent at that house. How their coming together had resulted in an explosion he'd never felt before. It took that one night for him to see Gail in a variety of lights and for him to realize she was someone he wanted to see again and again.

He'd had no idea what it would take to persuade her to see him again. By all rights, he should have told himself that night was just one of those things. Then he talked her into going out with him a second time to prove the first time was a fluke. Until he smelled her perfume and felt her lips against his. There was something deep within her that called to him. He was determined to find out just what that was.

Except their lives took an unexpected turn when Gail turned up pregnant.

He spoke the truth when he told her he wasn't angry

about the baby. Stunned, yes. He'd be the first to admit these things happen. He was fully prepared to do his part.

Gail might have the financial resources to raise a baby. And as a pediatrician, the baby would have excellent health care, but he could sense she didn't have the emotional skills to care for a baby. Not that she wasn't stable emotionally, but it was more she didn't *understand* children.

That's what he was here for.

He studied her as she ordered the shrimp, fries, salad and passion fruit iced tea.

"The same, but with the chowder and Coke," he told the waitress, handing her the menu. He waited until they were alone again. "I overreacted earlier. I should have had the sense to know you'd choose your doctor for his skills and not his looks. I guess if he wasn't a good physician no one would go to him, no matter who he looks like."

"I would think some men wouldn't like you treating their wives or girlfriends at an accident site," Gail said.

"I did get punched out once. The guy was drunk and thought I was copping a feel," Brian admitted. "He drove into a tree and ended up without a scratch while his girlfriend was badly injured. My partner dragged him off me before I ended up with more than a broken nose. What about you? Any of your patients' fathers develop a crush on you?"

"Not too much." She tore off another chunk of bread. "I suppose you'll want to be present when I have my sonogram."

Her usual tactic in changing subjects, he recognized. He was quickly discovering she didn't like to talk about herself. "I'd like to, yes. Some of the guys have been there and they said it's a pretty awesome experience."

She fiddled with her fork as her salad was placed in front of her.

"Then I'll make sure to arrange the appointment for when you're off duty."

"Thank you."

Brian kept conversation light and easy during their meal. He didn't miss the edgy motions Gail was making. What caused it? Then he realized she got that way every time he mentioned the baby. Was she having second thoughts? Were regrets starting to fill her mind?

"I—ah—I'll go with you to your parents' house this weekend," she said in a low voice after she pushed her empty dinner plate to one side. "After all, I should be with you when you tell them."

Brian grabbed hold of her hand, holding on tight when she tried to disengage.

"You're overwhelmed, aren't you? That's the whole problem. Why you act the way you do."

Gail looked at him, her mouth opening and closing as if she couldn't find the words to say.

How could he know? She'd hidden her feelings so well. At least, she thought she had.

She could feel the tears starting to prick her eyelids. The last thing she wanted to do was cry. It wasn't normally in her nature to cry, but a lot of things not normally in her nature seemed to be taking over lately.

There was no missing the way her lower lip trembled no matter how strongly she tried to stop it.

Brian uttered a soft curse and motioned for the waitress. He asked for the check and once received pulled out his wallet.

"This was my—" Gail's protest died off at the look he flashed her.

He held on to her arm as they left the restaurant and when he put his hand out for the keys, she handed them to him without any protest.

Brian adjusted the seat and rearview mirror and started up the engine. Before he put it in gear, he turned to her.

"Are you all right?"

The quietly asked question was enough to break through her tightly controlled emotions. The tears started rolling and didn't stop.

He took one look at her tearful face and wasted no time pulling her into his arms.

"Hey, it's going to be okay," he soothed.

"No, it's not!" she wailed, clutching him so hard he winced as her nails dug into his arms. "I have morning sickness twenty-four hours a day. None of my clothes fit. My face is blotchy, and my tummy pods out. I can't drink coffee anymore, I hate any kind of herbal tea and decaf coffee and for some reason chocolate gives me gas! Isn't that enough?"

Oh, boy! Brian felt totally out of his element. He'd delivered babies. But he hadn't been around much for what went on before the event. He racked his brain for anything his brothers and married friends said about their wives during their pregnancies. What little he remembered didn't help one bit.

"You can't worry about this, Gail. Your hormones are affecting your emotions right now." He fell back on the old standby. He pulled his handkerchief out of his pocket and dried the tears from her face. "I heard it gets easier."

She looked up with glistening eyes. "Really?" Her hushed voice begged for assurance.

"Really," he lied without a qualm.

Her lip started trembling again. "No, it won't. I don't know anything about raising a baby."

"Didn't you baby-sit when you were in high school?" He thought of his sisters making money every weekend.

Gail shook her head. "My spare time was spent studying or taking tennis and golf lessons."

"It's in the genes," he continued, desperate to say anything to calm her down. "Once you hold the baby you'll know exactly what to do."

"My mother didn't." She sniffled, snuggling in closer. "My genes lost that part."

Brian settled for just holding her and smoothing her hair back from her face. The clean scent of her hair teased his nostrils while the strands felt like silk against his fingers. He whispered soothing words in her ear, content with his lips barely touching her. He knew now was not the time to go any further.

As he again dried her tears, he couldn't help notice that Gail's classic features didn't take to tears well. Her eyes were red-rimmed and swollen, her face reddened and blotchy from crying.

She should have looked like a wet rag, not beautiful.

"Everyone has doubts," he said in a low voice. "I bet you had doubts your first day as an intern."

She sniffled and shook her head. "Medicine was what I wanted to practice, and I knew I could do it."

Was she always this self-assured? he asked himself. "Didn't you ever worry about anything?"

She shook her head again. "I wasn't brought up to

worry. Just to go and do what was required and do it well.''

He brushed her hair back from her forehead. The ends were damp from her tears.

''I'll drive you home.''

''No, you only need to take me back to the office. Your car is there.''

''I'll get it later. You're going home first.'' He started up the car.

Gail couldn't remember ever feeling this tired. She hadn't intended to voice her fears to Brian. He must think the worst of her now. Wondering what would happen now that he knew their child was in the hands of a woman who could treat children's ills but not their hearts.

She allowed him to drive her home. Lately, home seemed as good a hideaway as any.

They were both quiet as they entered the house. Gail watched Brian walk through the house, pause at the doorway to the guest room and move on.

''Since the alarm keypad doesn't indicate there's been an intruder, I don't think you'll find someone hiding in the closet,'' she told him.

''The alarm's a good thing,'' he said, tossing her keys up and down in his hand. ''I'm glad you have it. I'll need to use your car for a bit. I'll be back in a couple of hours.'' He stopped long enough to drop a kiss on her cheek.

She nodded. Just the touch of his mouth against her skin had her speechless. After Brian left, Gail got up and went to her bedroom to change her clothes. She put on her favorite robe and settled in the chair in the family room. She looked around, picturing the coffee table strewn with toys. Children's books scattered among her own reading material. She wouldn't do what her parents did, always ensuring books were returned to her room and never allowing toys to leave her room. She wanted her child to have more freedom than she had.

"Oh, baby," she said with a soft sigh, caressing her tummy. "I'll do my best. I promise. But you won't have to worry. You have a father who will easily do more than I could ever accomplish."

GAIL WAS ON THE PHONE counseling a patient's frantic mother when Brian returned.

"Yes, Mrs. Harris, I understand why you're worried about Jason," she said in a soothing voice. She looked up when she heard the sound of the garage door opening then soon saw Brian step inside. She noticed he'd changed into jeans and a T-shirt. Her gaze dropped to the duffel bag he carried then back up to his face. "But eating worms isn't deadly. For some reason small children think nothing of eating worms and snails. You yourself said your husband doesn't put any kind of poison out in the backyard, so you don't need to worry about that danger. I suggest you have a talk with Jason about what to eat and what not to." She listened to the woman's chatter while she watched Brian leave and bring in another bag. "Then have a talk with Parker, too. He needs to know that as an older brother, he can't urge his brother to eat worms and snails and dirt. If Jason vomits more than he should considering his diet, then call my service, and I'll meet you at the hospital. No, don't worry about it. Jason isn't the first to do this and I doubt he'll be the last. Goodbye." She disconnected the call. "People would think you're moving in."

"I am moving in." Brian brought in a third bag and set it down.

She could feel her jaw dropping in shock. "You can't do that!"

"Sure I can. I've got clean underwear." He gestured toward the three bags. "Clean shirts and socks. Don't worry. I pick up after myself. I don't leave hair in the sink, I remember to put the cap back on the toothpaste tube, and I don't snore. In some circles, I'm considered a prize catch."

"I don't care if you're considered the catch of the year. You can't stay here," she protested, hot on his heels as he strode down the hallway.

"You've got a guest room with its own bathroom, which is really nice, so there's no reason why I can't move in for a while" He dropped his bags onto the bed. He sat down and bounced experimentally. "Nice firm mattress. I like that." He patted the quilt. "Have a seat."

"I already know it's a firm mattress. And now that you know it, you can leave."

"Come on, Gail. Sit. Don't worry. I won't bite." He grinned, patting the quilt again.

She wasn't too sure about that. She gathered the folds of her robe in her hands and seated herself next to him.

Brian nodded as if she'd done the right thing. "You're worrying about things you don't need to worry about," he told her. "I've heard what your colleagues at the medical center have said about you and just now heard you talking to a patient's mom. The last thing you need to worry about is properly taking care of the baby. The only problem I can see is that you don't realize it. So, I'm here to teach you all you need to know about motherhood." Her eyes widened at his statement. "Except for breast feeding. If you plan to breast feed you'll have to go elsewhere for training. That's a skill way out of my league.''

''I'm glad to hear that,'' she snapped. She felt her life being taken out of her hands. ''But it doesn't mean you're staying here. My bursting into tears earlier is nothing unusual for a pregnant woman. My hormones are fluctuating. It's merely part of the process.'' Damn, she sounded like a medical journal!

''Then there's no reason why I can't be here to help you through all those fluctuating hormonal episodes.''

Why did she feel as if he were volunteering for much more than a position as roommate?

Brian got up and zipped open one of the bags. He pulled out underwear, socks and handkerchiefs, neatly piling them on the bed.

Gail couldn't help looking at the colorful array of cotton.

''You seem to like bright colors for your boxers,'' she mumbled.

''Yeah, I guess I do. I sleep in them during warm weather.'' He cast her a considering look. ''How about you?''

''I don't wear boxer shorts,'' she said tartly.

''Glad to hear it. Then I don't have to worry about you trying to steal mine.'' He opened a drawer and placed them inside. Another bag yielded T-shirts and jeans. ''I go back on duty in two days, but you won't have to worry about anything. I'm adaptable. I'm going to take a closer look at your garage door opener. It seems to hang up a little when it's going up.''

With every item he put away, she could see her life spiraling more and more out of control.

''You can't live here.'' Gail was certain she sounded like a broken record.

"We have a lot to do in the next six months, and it will be a lot easier if we're sharing the same quarters during that time. Besides, you should have someone around when it gets closer to the time. And I want to be your birthing coach. Which means we need to attend classes."

Her hackles were raising big time now. "I already know how to breathe properly!"

"It's different when you're in labor. I know some of the basics from helping women, but now we're talking about you, and I want to know everything. I meant it when I said I wanted to be with you all the way, Gail." There was no laughter in his eyes, only deep sincerity that turned them a dark cobalt color.

He walked over to her and cupped her chin with his hand. He tipped it upward.

"We're in this together, kid."

She groaned and shut her eyes. "I'm crazy to even think of doing this."

"It'll all work out. You'll see."

At that moment, she wasn't sure his assurance was what she needed.

"You clean up after yourself, if you make a mess in the kitchen you clean it yourself and you have to do your own laundry."

He held her hands up and pressed a kiss against each palm. His lips lingered against the second palm. "You won't regret it," he murmured against her skin.

Gail was already regretting it, but it was too late for her to take back her words. She never thought of herself as an impulsive person. Allowing Brian to stay in her home was about one of the most impulsive actions she'd made lately. Right next to her pregnancy.

Something else to blame on the hormones.

If she wasn't careful, pretty soon she'd be blaming the weather on her hormones.

Chapter Ten

"Medical school didn't tell me how much a stomach could hate a person," Gail moaned, staggering from the bathroom back into her bedroom. She collapsed on the bed with one arm flung over her face. "Patients I saw during my OB rotation talked about this, but I thought they were exaggerating. Ha! They didn't tell the half of it."

"Here. I brought you some crackers and ginger tea." Brian helped her sit up then lifted the cup to her lips. "Just sip it slowly. Your stomach should calm down pretty soon."

She wrinkled her nose as the spicy aroma wafted upward. She feared her stomach would start its rock-and-roll gyrations again, but luckily it remained quiet. "I don't want to drink anything. I've been sick enough today."

"You don't have to smell it. Just drink it," he said patiently. "You didn't want the medication the doctor gave you, and you need something. Abby said ginger is good for nausea. Just try one little sip. Good. Now try another. Once your stomach's settled down, you can try a little breakfast. You'll be feeling fine by the time we leave for Mom and Dad's barbecue."

She closed her eyes. The thought of going anywhere, especially his parents' house, was daunting. The idea of staying home, staying in bed was comforting. "I think I'd better stay home. Riding in the car might not help my nausea."

"Sure it will. You need to be out in the fresh air."

Gail already knew that voice. Brian used it when he wouldn't allow her to back out of something. Just as he did the night he suggested they go to his gym and work out. She balked at the idea, even argued with him, but he refused to take no for an answer. Before she knew it, she was a member at the fitness center, and she was set up with a program suited for her needs. Brian alternately bullied and coaxed her into going with him nights he was off duty.

For a man who seemed so easygoing, he could be stubborn when he wanted. And one thing he was stubborn about was taking care of her. Whether she wanted him to or not.

He ignored the fact she was a physician and had the knowledge to do what was necessary. He ignored the fact that she'd been taking care of herself for many years now without any problems. He adjusted the garage door opener so it opened and closed smoothly the way it should. She didn't have to worry about taking the trash out because he took it out without her having to say anything about it. She never saw one stray piece of clothing marring the guest bedroom carpet. A peek into his bathroom showed no globs of toothpaste decorating the sink, and she hadn't seen the seat left up once.

She sipped the tea because it was easier than having to listen to Brian sweet-talk her into drinking it. This morning, she wished he'd bully her. Then she could fight back and have a reason for feeling cranky. But when he was so sweet and understanding, she could only give in so he would stop being so darn helpful!

Damn him. The tea did settle her stomach.

She didn't want to go to his parents' house. Family gatherings had never been a part of her childhood. Holiday dinners had always been eaten at restaurants because her mother didn't want to be bothered with all the work of putting together a special dinner. Her grandparents didn't tolerate children any more than her parents did, so a neutral meeting place was better. There was a time when young Gail wondered how the adults managed to have sex enough to make a child when *affection* didn't appear to be a word in their vocabulary. She grew up thinking affection wasn't allowed, and even now, she couldn't display it to anyone.

Her time with Brian warned her that his family would be the exact opposite. She could see them hugging and kissing each other at the drop of a hat. And because she'd stand back, they'd probably view her as some kind of oddity. They'd naturally wonder why Brian would bother with a cold fish like her. The description was nothing new. The first time she'd heard it was from a date when she was in medical school. He'd actually told her she would be an excellent case study for frigidity. She showed him the door and spent the night refusing to cry because she knew crying denoted weakness.

The past few months taught her that crying was something she'd have to get used to for the next five months or so. John told her some women suffered it throughout their pregnancy. Gail feared she was going to be one of those women.

"I'M GOING for a run," Brian announced, startling her out of her introspection.

She looked up and nodded as he headed out the back door with a wave of the hand over his shoulder. Seeing him in an oversize tank top and running shorts wasn't a new sight. He enjoyed running in the nearby park and tried to do it every day he was off duty. She'd been coerced into going with him once, but she kept a more sedate pace. But it didn't stop her from noticing how women noticed Brian.

As if they could ignore him with his lean runner's build, blue eyes and broad smile flashing against his tanned features. Even she couldn't help feeling a little tipsy in her stomach when she looked at him.

Everyone at the center told her he was a prime catch. Sheila broadly hinted that he was perfect husband material and that she should not let him get away.

She didn't want to get married. She didn't want a relationship. She wouldn't be any good at it anyway. After all, she was a product of her parents, and they were the coldest people she'd ever known.

But she felt a child should know its father. She wanted her baby to have the family she didn't have while she was growing up. She knew with Brian the baby would have that family.

What she didn't need was Brian as a roommate.

Not that that would have stopped him. He was determined to stay here during her pregnancy.

This afternoon was going to be a disaster. She just knew it.

And it wasn't just because her stomach started acting up again.

"DON'T LET THEM try to bowl you over. They don't mean to, but sometimes it happens," Brian advised during the drive to his parents' house. "Of course, Mom will take you under her wing. That's always her way. And she'll keep everyone in line. Especially my brothers.'' He grinned. ''They're more scared of her than they are of me.''

Gail could already feel her stomach doing somersaults. She thought she'd done everything right. She pulled her hair back into a ponytail and chose a pair of comfortable navy twill shorts and a lemon-colored polo shirt. She studied herself in the mirror and wondered if she was overdressed. She was convinced of it when Brian came out of the guest room wearing a tank top with the fire department logo emblazoned on the front and cutoff denims. His running shoes equally looked ready for the rag bag. Since she couldn't imagine going anywhere dressed so casually, she could only pray the women would be better dressed.

As he drove, Brian flashed her a quick look. There was no denying the signs. Her hands twisted and turned in her lap. She stared straight ahead as if the bumper of the Toyota a short distance in front of them held all the answers. Even though she spent a great deal of time in the bathroom putting on makeup, her face was still pale. And she hadn't said more than three words since they'd left the house.

If he didn't know any better, he'd say she was scared to death.

The idea of anyone being scared of his family was laughable. Not that he dared laugh at her fears. She owned at least one scalpel and knew how to use it.

His first thought was to get her to laugh. But her tight features warned him it wouldn't be a good idea. But he had to do something to take her mind off fears she didn't need.

He pulled over to the side of the road and allowed the engine to idle.

Gail swiveled her head. "What's wrong?" Her voice was high-pitched and taut.

"Nothing." He rested his right arm along the back of her seat and allowed his hand to dangle over her shoulder. "I thought we'd sit here a few minutes and enjoy the view."

She looked around at what had to have been miles of lush, green pasture. Some corrals were filled with scattered cattle and others with horses grazing. The air was hot and dry with the sun burning overhead. No one else was in sight once the Toyota turned off the main road a few miles back.

"So which do your parents have? Cattle or horses?" she asked.

"Neither. They used to say we were animals enough for them. They have five acres, but Dad seems to have used up most of it." He shifted his hand so he could rub the back of her neck. It was knotted tight with tension that he attempted to rub loose. When that didn't seem to work, he decided there was only one way to get her mind off her fears. In one smooth move he leaned over and used his hand to keep her chin still. Her lips parted in a silent O as he covered them.

In those first seconds he tasted her surprise, savored her astonishment, and just plain feasted on the woman who was better than any alcohol. Gail's soft moan filled his mouth just before he moved his mouth along the corners of her lips before returning to her mouth that was as tantalizing as a fine wine.

It would have been easy to spend the rest of the day reacquainting himself with her mouth. He would have gladly ignored his arousal that felt more uncomfortable by the moment as long as he could keep on kissing her. And she kept on responding. By the time he pulled back, her eyes were glazed and her face flushed. She looked well kissed, but even more important, she looked relaxed. Too bad he hadn't thought of this earlier.

"I guess we'd better get going. We don't want them sending out a search party," he said huskily. He still didn't make a move to put the car in gear.

"Hmm?" she asked, still lost. She abruptly shook her head to help her return to her senses. She quickly pulled down the visor and used the mirror there to reapply her lip gloss.

Brian watched her, entranced by the everyday sight of her coloring her lips. He smiled. The tension was gone.

A few miles down, he pulled off the main road and drove through an open gate. A mailbox designed to look like an Edsel sat out front with Walker painted on the license plate.

"Everyone else around here has mailboxes designed to look like cows or horses, but Dad said it just didn't work for him. When Mom raised goats he said no way would he have a goat mailbox," he explained, as he drove up the winding driveway that boasted lush green grass on either side. She couldn't imagine anything less than a tractor keeping the lawn in check.

"So, what did he have?" Gail asked, intrigued by his story.

He grinned, not aware his grin caused her senses to teeter-totter. "For quite a few years we had a mailbox that was painted to resemble a jail. It said Walker Penitentiary."

"How eccentric," she said for lack of anything else.

"Around here, my family is about as normal as you can get."

Gail saw what looked like a small parking lot off to the side. She doubted most of the cars were less than twenty-five years old, but all of them gleamed with what had to be fresh coats of wax and looked in excellent condition. Her gaze shifted right toward the house. The two-story soft-gray house with colonial-blue trim looked like something out of a magazine. Flowers and shrubs lent riots of color along the front of the house.

"How many brothers and sisters did you say you have?" she asked.

The panic in her voice must have alerted him.

"Four. None of them are insane, psychotic or have multiple personalities. As least, that's what we tell ourselves." He climbed out and walked around to the passenger door. He grasped Gail's hand and helped her out.

She didn't mind that he kept hold of her hand as they started up the brick walkway that was lined with brightly colored flowers. Before they could reach the front door, it opened and a woman stepped outside.

There was no doubt she was Brian's mother because she had the same blue eyes as her son, and while her hair had lightened with time, Gail sensed at one time it had been the same deep-brown as Brian's had been. The short-sleeved, ribbed-cotton tunic and pink floral pants on her petite figure were perfect for the hot weather.

"About time you got here," she scolded Brian as he kissed her on the cheek, and she responded in kind. She turned to Gail with a warm smile. "And you must be Gail. I'm Cathy."

"I'm pleased to meet you, Mrs. Walker," she said, hoping her smile didn't wobble as she felt it did.

"Cathy," she corrected, hugging Gail. "Although

you'll quickly learn I answer to a lot of names around here.'' She kept her hands on Gail's arms as she leaned back and studied her. "If God is on our side, the baby will have your looks and smarts. The last thing this world needs is another Brian. If you will do this one thing for me, I will love you forever.''

Gail was afraid she looked like a fish with her mouth opening and closing but no words came out.

"C'mon Mom, you'll scare her," Brian teased, taking each of them by the arm and walking up to the door. "How about something cold to drink?"

"You know where the beer is and there's plenty of iced tea and soda.'' She glanced at Gail. "Still have the nausea?''

She nodded. She didn't think Brian's parents knew about her pregnancy! She thought they were going to tell them together. Yet it was obvious, his mother already knew. And now Gail was expected to discuss it with a woman she'd only just met. Especially when the woman was the mother of the father of Gail's child. What must she think of Gail? Gail needed to get Brian alone and find out how his mother knew about her pregnancy.

Cathy tsked. "Why some go through all nine months losing their lunch on a regular basis and others don't have a twinge, I'll never know. With each of my children, I threw up like clockwork every morning at eight. Just the one time and that was it. But if you talk to Abby, Jeff's wife, she'll tell you her morning sickness would last all night." She led them through the cool interior of the house where Gail caught glimpses of furniture chosen for comfort instead of style. She put her sunglasses back on when they stepped back into the sun.

Gail pulled back on Brian's hand before they reached the door.

"You told them?" she demanded in a harsh whisper. "How could you do that?"

He hesitated. "I thought maybe it would be better to do it ahead of time than just making an announcement here. I stopped by here last night and told them."

She wanted to kill him. "And you didn't think to tell me before we arrived? Do you know how I felt when she mentioned it?"

He shifted under her gaze. There was no doubt he was in trouble. "I thought I was making it easier."

Gail glared at him. "Guess what? You didn't." She headed for the patio door and thrust it open.

The moment they left the house, Gail felt as if she'd been thrust into a human zoo. It wasn't just the adults who left her speechless, but the sight of so many children running around. A circular playpen had been set up under a large tree with a couple of babies peacefully sleeping, and toddlers only had to approach any adult to be picked up, hugged and kissed.

"Toto, you are way out of your league here," she whispered to herself, blindly reaching out to grip Brian's hand so hard he winced. She probably cut off the circulation. She didn't care. She was still angry at him but that didn't mean she'd let him abandon her! Judging from the encouraging squeeze he gave back, he understood her thoughts.

"Hey, Pops!" one man shouted, lifting his beer in a salute. He disengaged himself from the group and walked over to them. "About time you showed up."

No doubt he was one of Brian's brothers. He had the same blue eyes, good looks and body no woman would turn down. And while he looked enough like Brian to be his twin, she could have been blindfolded and still known the difference in the dark.

"Jeff, what happened to you?" Brian gestured to the white bandage circling his brother's dark forearm.

Jeff made a face. "I was working on Carrie's bike, and the wrench slipped. Abby said I have more accidents at home then I do at work."

"You do," Brian agreed with a broad grin. "There's a good reason why Mark and I come over every Christmas Eve to put together the kids' toys." He turned to Gail. "Jeff put together a dollhouse once for the girls. It was a sorry sight. It took Mark and I a couple of hours to fix it. Gail, this is my oldest brother, Jeff. The hot-looking blonde over there is his wife, Abby, and the twin terrors in pink are their daughters, Casey and Carrie."

"Hello, Gail." Jeff's smile was eerily like his brother's. "It's a shame you had to settle for the ugliest of the family."

"Yeah, when you could have had me." Mark ambled over and greeted Gail with a hug and kiss on the cheek. "Good to see you again, Doc. You look better than the last time I saw you."

Gail blushed as she remembered the time she first met Brian's brother.

Before she knew it, five other men had come up and introduced themselves, all telling her she'd be better off with them instead of Brian. They all offered to enlighten her to Brian's bad habits and their good ones.

"Great. Just what the woman wants. Sweaty men surrounding her until she can't think. Do any of you have a brain in your heads?" Abby scolded, plowing her way through. She rolled her eyes at the predictable rude comments that followed. She grabbed Gail's hand and pulled her away from the group. "Don't let them scare you.

When all these guys get together, it's like something out of *Animal House*. We sane ones usually just sit back and hope the police don't show up.'' She guided her over to the group of women who sat in patio chairs by the large swimming pool that was filled with quite a few small children and even a couple of teenagers. A heavily pregnant German shepherd lay panting nearby. ''And don't worry, we won't pester you for free medical advice. We made a pact not to ask for free medical advice. But I do admit I'm looking for a new pediatrician, and I did hear good things about you.''

''Who are you with now?'' Gail asked, still a bit dazed at the way these people accepted her so naturally. It didn't help that Abby looked like the poster girl for California Beach with her golden-blond hair flowing down her back in easy waves. Her white tank top with a hint of lace at the neckline and white shorts showcased a slim figure that would make a model proud. Gail was certain she would have hated this woman if she wasn't so friendly.

Abby wrinkled her nose. ''Dr. Loren Baxter.''

Gail didn't say anything, but she could guess why Abby wasn't happy with the man. She heard he was an excellent physician but that he tended to act condescendingly to parents, and mothers usually received a paternal pat on the head. Since she'd always been taught when she couldn't say something nice to not say anything at all, she wisely kept silent.

Abby stopped and grasped Gail's arm. ''Just please tell me you're taking new patients,'' she pleaded. ''I understand you're probably going to want to cut down because of your pregnancy, but I can promise you my kids are rarely sick. I'd just feel better knowing I can take them to someone else. I'm five months along, so there will be a third there at some time.''

Gail stared at her with disbelief. "You're pregnant?" She couldn't see a sign the woman was expecting.

Abby laughed. "Yes, I know I don't look it. Even carrying twins I didn't start to really show until my sixth month. Then I suddenly blew up like a beach ball. In a few weeks, you won't even recognize me."

"Here I can't get into a lot of my clothes since they're tailored," Gail said ruefully. "Call my office for an appointment when you're ready to change."

Abby brightened. "Oh, I will." She stopped at the edge of the group. "A new member, ladies. This is Gail, Brian's girlfriend."

"Oh, I'm not—" Gail stopped. How was she supposed to describe herself? That they didn't date, weren't in a relationship, but they were living together without sleeping together, and she was having his child. She had no idea how that would describe her.

"This is Stacy, she's Rick's girlfriend. Marie who came with Kurt. Ginna's Brian's older sister, Barbara's married to Matt, and Nikki over there is the baby of the family." Each responded with a smile and wave. "I decided I'd rescue her from the men before she decided we were all crazy. Diet Coke or iced tea?" She turned to Gail.

"Diet Coke." She accepted an ice-filled glass. "Thank you."

"So, tell me." Nikki leaned forward, a look of anticipation on her face. "Why exactly did you choose Brian from all those hunks on the wall?"

Gail almost choked on her drink. "His picture was at eye level," she finally managed to say.

Nikki laughed delightedly. "I love it! That should

keep his ego in check.'' With her short and feathery
dark-brown hair framing delicate features and the same
blue eyes, she was the feminine version of her brothers.
Gail noticed even some of her hand gestures mimicked
her brothers. Dressed in faded denim shorts and a green
cotton halter top with a great deal of tanned skin showing in between, she was the picture of health.

She noticed Ginna had the same family good looks.
But while Brian and Jeff were pure masculinity, like
Nikki, Ginna was feminine to the core. Her white mini
floral print sundress that bared her arms and shoulders
suited her. Her dark hair flowed down her back in spiral
curls, lending a touch of wildness to her demeanor.

Gail racked her memory to recall where she'd seen
the woman before. It took a moment for her to place
Brian's sister. ''You work at Steppin' Out, don't you?''

Ginna nodded. ''I do hair there. You see Holly, don't
you?''

Gail nodded. ''I've gone to her for the past few
years.''

''Don't you love going there?'' Nikki asked, almost
bouncing in her chair. Her energy level was such that
she didn't appear to sit still for too long. ''I'm always
going in for a facial or massage. I'm also a sucker for
their spa pedicures.'' She wiggled her shimmering
peach-polished toes. ''Karen gives this incredible foot
and leg massage. I feel so relaxed after it that I want to
be carried out so I don't ruin my pretty new feet.'' She
giggled.

All it took was her comment to inspire everyone to
share what feature they enjoyed most at the day spa and
salon. As Gail listened to the animated talk going back
and forth she realized they'd easily included her in their
group and acted as if they'd always known her.

She realized before she'd always been introduced as Dr. Gail Roberts and here, Abby only used her first name. For once, she was treated as Gail, a woman and not Gail, a doctor. She blamed her hormones on the tears that threatened to fall.

She didn't turn around when a pair of warm hands settled on her shoulders.

"What insidious plots against mankind have you all come up with?" Brian asked, standing behind Gail as he kneaded her shoulders.

"As if we'd tell you, you man, you," Abby scoffed. "The first thing you'd do is run and tell the others."

"I'm taking my lady away. I want to show Gail the garage," he announced.

The women looked at each other with raised eyebrows.

"The inner sanctum," Ginna said with teasing reverence.

Gail gulped. "Inner sanctum?"

"They're just jealous because they're not invited." Brian grabbed her hand and pulled her out of her chair. He kept his fingers laced through hers as he made an elaborate bow to the group. "Ladies, I'm stealing my woman away for a little while. Probably just as well since I'm sure some of you are filling her head with horrifying and untrue tales about me."

Ginna leaned back in her chair with one hand lifted languidly. "Darn. And here I was just getting to that lovely story of when you were five and decided you wanted to be mud boy. You remember, don't you, Brian? You took off all your clothes, hosed yourself down then rolled in the dirt. Such an attractive picture." She suddenly stood up. "In fact, didn't Mom take a picture? I'm sure it's in one of the photo albums."

"Okay, okay." Brian backed off quickly. "We don't need to go into such things. Unless—" a wicked gleam entered his eyes "—there was that time Kirk Jackson brought you home from the homecoming dance, and you didn't come in right away and Dad caught you two—"

"Go!" she ordered haughtily. "Go now and you will live."

Brian sketched another bow as he pulled Gail off with him.

"My sister has always enjoyed bringing out the family skeletons. I figured the least I could do was return in kind," he told her as he led her up a path covered with decorative paving stones.

"Are you going to explain what the inner sanctum is?" she asked, pulling back on his hand so he would realize she wanted to walk at a slower pace.

"Nah. It's something you have to see."

Gail looked at the sprawling at the end of the path. "It doesn't look like a barn," she decided. "Not that it would, since you said your parents don't keep cattle or horses."

"It houses something that doesn't require regular feeding." As they reached the building, the sound of metal hitting metal punctuated by sporadic curses grew louder. "And it is very special." He walked around until they faced the other side with rolled up doors opened to the light. "Lady on the deck!" he shouted.

Gail knew very little about cars other than what she read in *Consumer Reports,* but she could tell the vehicles housed in the building were classics of more than thirty years and were in various stages of repair. The two men walking toward her were dressed in coveralls dotted with grease and dirt. One, even with silvery hair, showed Brian's height and strong features and showed her what

Brian would look like in thirty years. The other man, his own hair white and face creased from time and weather and his figure stooped a bit from age, revealed Brian's heritage.

"Gail, this is my dad, Lou, and my granddad, Theo," Brian's voice was filled with love for the two men. "And what you see behind them is their kingdom. Out here is the beginning of Walker Auto Repair when it opened more than sixty years ago. They hoped one of us would follow their footsteps, but it was soon apparent, that sad to say, we can't even change the oil in our cars without making a major mess."

"Hell, we don't even let the boy take a spark plug out of the box," Lou said in a gravelly voice. His smile touched his eyes as he looked at Gail. "I'd hug you, gal, but I don't think you'd appreciate this crud on your pretty clothes."

"When're the two of you getting married?" Theo asked in a booming voice not diminished by age.

"Gramps..." Brian muttered in silent warning even though he doubted his grandfather would heed it.

Gail stiffened. "Because of my baby, you mean," she challenged.

"You call it your baby, but Brian was there, too." He speared Brian with blue eyes that flashed animation.

"I call it *my* baby because *I'm* the one carrying it, and *I'm* the one who will be going through labor to bring this child into the world," she replied. "Cathy said she hopes I have a girl because there are too many Walker men in this world. I can see she's right. More females are definitely needed."

Brian turned away, coughing into his closed fist to hide his laughter. He noticed his dad standing a bit behind his grandfather was looking off into space. Gail and his grandfather were still involved in a staring contest, and it looked like neither would be backing down any time soon.

Then, just as suddenly as it started, the tension lessened. Theo's face creased in a broad smile, and he reached over and kissed her on the cheek. He then turned to Brian.

"She'll do."

"I'd be careful if I were you, Grandpa. Gram sees you kissing other women she'll give you some major whoopass," Brian teased, keeping an arm possessively around Gail's shoulders. "Jeff's fired up the barbecue. Mom said you need to come on back in time to clean up."

"Maybe Gail wants to see the operation first," Lou suggested.

She looked over the cars lying in various stages of work. "So you're a mechanic?" she asked, then grew a little miffed at Brian's laughter.

"Sweetheart, my dad and granddad are artists in their own right," he explained. "No one knows classic cars inside and out the way these two do. They can listen to an engine and tell you exactly what's wrong with it. Car owners come from three and four states away for them to work on their cars. They also do renovations. Pick up what looks like a piece of junk and turn it into a piece of art." He gestured toward a Ford Woody station wagon. "The ultimate surfermobile."

"What kind of car do you drive?" Theo asked.

"I had a BMW convertible until it was carjacked," she explained. "I presently have a Maxima."

Theo looked her over then turned to Brian. "With her pregnant, something sturdy. An SUV is always good with the custom baby seat installed. None of those mini-vans though. Too yuppie.''

"Thank you, I think.'' She glared at him, not appreciating his thinking she would allow him to take over her life for her. She wondered if Brian's moving in with her was merely the beginning. Would he start thinking he knew better than her? If so, he'd learn differently really fast!

"All right, hot stuff.'' Brian tugged on her hand. "Let's go back and get some food into you before you start chewing on them.''

"He started it!'' she protested as he pulled her away. The sound of the men's laughter followed them.

"It's just the way he is. He approves of you,'' he told her, wrapping an arm around her shoulders as they walked.

Gail looked down at the ground because it was easier than risking Brian see her thoughts. Deep down she was furious the men seemed to think they knew how she should handle her life. And her mode of transportation. At the same time, she was touched they so readily welcomed her. His father appeared to be a sweetheart, and his grandfather was the typical ornery sort you had to love. There was nothing standoffish about the Walker men. Not like the Roberts clan who always felt they were heads and shoulders above the rest of the world.

As a child, she wondered many times what it would be like to have a real family surround her where everyone hugged everyone else. A family like she'd seen on television.

Now that she'd discovered reality, she was quickly discovering it was very scary. And very nice.

Chapter Eleven

Cathy deftly separated Gail from Brian and urged her into the kitchen to help with final meal preparations. Cathy sat her at the table and put her to work tearing lettuce for a green salad while she supervised Ginna and Abby in carrying condiments and other salads outside.

Gail was certain Cathy arranged it so they would be left alone for a while.

Now comes the interrogation. She almost shredded the lettuce into tiny bits as she tensely waited.

"That looks fine," Cathy took the bowl from her and set it to one side. She sat on the stool next to Gail. "So, tell me how my son managed to find someone who has both brains and beauty. And I'm certain there's common sense mixed in there."

"Too bad the men in your family don't prize common sense. Your father-in-law is hoping for another boy," Gail said dryly. "I can't imagine that would be a good idea."

Cathy's laughter was light and musical. "Theo's bark has always been worse than his bite. He claims boys are his favorites, but it's his daughters and granddaughters who've always been able to wrap him around their little fingers. The man is pure marshmallow inside. He just doesn't like to show it." She pulled the cutting board toward her and began deftly slicing tomatoes. "The first time I met him he told me my hips were too narrow for childbearing. I told him he should worry more about his son's part in the process, and I'd worry about my hips."

Gail's lips quivered. "I told him I was carrying the baby and not Brian."

Cathy smiled. "Good for you. You do understand Theo. He loves nothing more than a woman putting him in his place."

Her own smile dimmed. She didn't want the older woman thinking there would be more there than there was.

"Cathy, I told Brian I wouldn't marry him because of the baby. Not that he came out and asked me. But I wanted him to know that right off, so there wouldn't be any misunderstandings. To begin with, we don't know each other well enough to even think long-term. Not to mention I'm not good in a relationship," she reluctantly imparted then thought to add, "but I want the baby to know his or her family. I would never deny you that. I know how important family is to Brian. I want his child to have a sense of family. I'm glad that you're so willing to accept the baby. I'm also putting Brian's name on the birth certificate."

Cathy's serene smile didn't change. "You poor dear. You thought we would burn you at the stake because you wouldn't consider marrying our son. One thing Lou and I try to do is not interfere in our children's lives. After all, why should everyone be unhappy because you rushed into something that didn't work out? I am glad you are willing to share the baby with us. There's nothing I like better than to play the doting grandmother. I only hope you're ready for lots of advice on pregnancy and motherhood because that is one thing you'll receive. Everything else is up to you and Brian to work out."

"Can you persuade him he doesn't need to stay with me?" she pleaded. Unwilling to sit there and do nothing, she added shredded carrots to the lettuce while Cathy threw in the tomatoes.

"He must feel you need someone there," she pointed out. "And it doesn't sound as if you tried to lock him out."

"Brian's like those pesky flies you get during the summer. Once they get in the house you just can't get them out."

"Then I hope that particular pesky fly is remembering everything I taught him."

"So far he is, but the day he isn't is the day I'm getting out some nasty bug spray," Gail said with feeling.

"SHE'S DEFINITELY good-looking, old buddy." Kurt clapped Brian on the back. "Never knew kids were lucky enough to have doctors looking like her. So, when are you following in your brother's footsteps and traveling the married path?"

"Gail doesn't want to get married." The confession tasted like acid in his mouth. Even a slug of beer didn't wash it away.

"And you do? The man who only went out on a date because his sister put his picture up on a dating bulletin board?" Jeff flipped steaks and hamburgers on the large barbecue grill.

"Nikki thought I needed a social life."

"That the best you can come up with?"

Brian set his bottle to one side. "That's my answer and I'm sticking to it."

"Then you've lost your touch with words, my boy." Lou stood on the other side of the grill. "You are going to marry her before the baby is born, aren't you? A child needs two parents who are joined together in matrimony."

Brian expelled a low-voiced curse. One that would have had his mouth washed out with soap if his mother had heard him.

His father's sharp gaze could have sliced steel. A silent warning to be respectful.

"Gail doesn't want to get married. And I'm not going to push her. In one way, she's right. We don't really don't know each other and we need to do that," he said slowly. "For now, it's enough she's letting me stick around, and she's not shutting me out of the baby's life."

"You knew each other well enough to make a baby."

The other men would have snickered at Brian's expense, except, at one time or another each of them had been under fire and listened to the older man's lectures in the past. Brian and Jeff might have been the only ones of Lou's blood, but any of the men knew they'd get the proverbial slap upside the head if they were out of line.

"Then get to know the lady better on an intellectual level," Mark advised. "You're living with her. You've got the time."

Brian didn't take his eyes off his brother. "The steaks are done."

He watched Gail leave the kitchen in his mother's company. A warm rush of pleasure flooded through his body as he noticed both were smiling.

Maybe it wouldn't be so difficult to convince her after all.

"THERE'S TOO MUCH food here," Gail protested at the laden plate Brian brought her.

"I forgot some of Ginna's pasta salad. Come on, thug, go bother someone else," he ordered an eight-year-old David who'd been sitting next to Gail.

"She said I can sit next to her," he informed the man.

"Yeah, well, if you want to play on my team after lunch, you'll hit the road." Brian cocked his thumb over his shoulder.

David stood up and promptly walked around to Gail's other side. He glared at Brian.

"She's a kid's doctor," Brian told him. "She'll give you shots in the butt. She'll see you naked."

David smiled beatifically at Gail. "That's okay."

Gail couldn't hold back a chuckle. "All right, you two. I prefer to eat my meal in peace."

"David's a thug," Brian announced. "He's only happy when he's pestering his little sister."

"Brian." Gail laid her free hand on his arm. She leaned forward so she could whisper in his ear. "He's only eight years old. It's in his nature. And right now, he's doing a wonderful job of yanking your chain."

He forked a piece of steak into his mouth. David looked at him and crossed his eyes.

"You keep on doing that and they'll stay that way forever," he told the boy.

"I'm glad to see you interact so well with small children," she said in a low voice, but a hint of a smile flirted with her lips.

"I've been told it's because I never grew up."

"That I can understand," she murmured. She had barely nibbled at half of what was on her plate when she put her plate to one side. "Don't say anything about eating for two," she told him when he looked at her plate then swung his gaze back to her. "You gave me enough food for twice that number of people."

His gaze softened as he looked at her. He brushed her cheek with the back of his fingertips.

"Are you doing okay? I guess I did throw you into the lions' den, so to speak."

"Hearing about it and seeing it for myself are two entirely different things," she admitted. "But I'll survive."

"We're playing touch football after we eat," Jeff called over. "You up to it?"

Brian didn't take his eyes off Gail. She smiled.

"Go ahead, big boy. Show me your stuff."

"Too bad we don't have one of those cute little cropped sweaters and short skirts for you to wear, so you could properly cheer me on."

"Dream on, little boy."

Brian made sure Gail was comfortable in a patio chair before loping off to join his brothers and friends.

"This is their chance to pretend they're macho men while we sit here and ooh and ahh over them," Abby said, pulling up a chair next to Gail. "It's a relatively painless process, and it makes them feel like hot stuff for a while." She half turned in her chair so she could face Gail. "This is all new to you, isn't it? Didn't your family have barbecues and such?"

"Not if they could help it," she admitted. "I don't think my parents got along well with either set of grandparents and vice versa." She surprised herself with her confession since she didn't like to talk about her family. She wasn't sure if it was the air or just the people who showed their sincere interest that prompted her to say more than she had in years.

Abby reached over and patted her hand. "I'd say

you're due for a treat around here. Cathy and Lou are fantastic. There are no in-laws here, just family. The first thing they tell you is they won't meddle and believe me, they don't. But they're there for you, and if one of their own is in the wrong, they're the first to say so. Of course, I've known them since I was in grade school. I went to school with Brian and had a crush on Jeff for what had seemed like forever before he finally noticed me. Then it still took some heavy-duty plotting to get him to ask me out. He'd always thought of me as his little brother's friend. Amazing what a hot-pink bikini can do to change a guy's mind.'' She chuckled. She glanced toward the field. ''Good catch, hot stuff!'' she shouted, clapping loudly. Jeff looked her way and flashed her a grin. ''See? You throw them a bone and they're happy.''

Gail was too engrossed watching Brian. He'd stripped off his shirt and tossed it to one side. His tanned skin gleamed with sweat from his exertions as he zigzagged his way down the field for a touchdown. Before he could reach his goal, he was tackled by Mark and soon lay under a pile of men. She started to rise, fearing he was hurt until they all stood up and Kurt helped Brian up. She collapsed against her chair as she realized he was all right.

The football game she watched was nothing like the games she'd seen on television. These men bent the rules to their advantage and seemed to enjoy tackling each other more than running with the ball to the goal line. By the time the game was finished, all the men were filthy but pleased with themselves.

Brian snatched up his shirt on the way over to where Gail and Abby sat. He wiped his face clean as he walked toward her. Gail let out a soft shriek when he picked her up in his arms, spinning her around as he planted a kiss on her mouth.

"Hey, babe, we won!"

"Brian!" She gripped his shoulders. "Turning me into a merry-go-round is not a good idea!"

He stopped abruptly. "Oh, honey, I'm sorry." He carefully set her back down on her feet. "Are you okay?"

She mentally tallied the state of her stomach and decided it was still stable. "Yes, but I don't want to take any chances."

"Don't even think about it," Abby warned her husband when he came up. "No way I want that filth on my clothes."

Gail remained in the circle of Brian's arms. He was sweaty and dirty, but she felt she needed the support.

"Tired?" He brushed his lips against her ear.

She nodded.

"We're outta here," he announced, keeping one arm around her shoulders.

He overrode her protests and guided her back to the patio. Cathy sat there with several people.

"Thanks for a great day, Mom." He kissed her on the cheek. "I'm going to take Gail home while she still has good thoughts about us."

"I'm glad you could come, dear," Cathy told her after hugging her. "Don't be a stranger. You don't need Brian to come out here. In fact, leave him home. I'll send Lou somewhere and we can have a good talk." She patted Gail's hand.

"Sneaking off without saying goodbye?" Theo walked over. His dark brows furrowed as he gazed at them.

"Sure am, before you decide to kidnap my lady,"

Brian told him. "Grams wouldn't be too happy if you tried to bring a new woman into the house."

"A doctor in the house is always handy," he rumbled.

"Yeah, one would be handy to patch you up after Grams takes a shotgun after you," Brian teased. "Tell Grams we'll see her next time."

"She's supposed to get back from that blasted cruise next week."

Gail and Brian left, with Gail loaded down with phone numbers and promises to call for lunch or shopping. Once she was settled in the passenger seat of Brian's 'Vette, she felt ready for a nap.

"Your family is very nice," she said sleepily, resting her head against the seat.

"I'm glad you think so." Brian started up the car.

By the time they reached the main road, Gail was asleep. She slept so heavily she didn't stir when Brian parked the car in the garage and carried her into the house.

He placed her on the couch in the family room and covered her with an afghan.

"Brian?" Gail's voice was slurred with sleep.

"Go back to sleep," he said softly.

"I had a nice day," she said before she rolled onto her side and fell back asleep.

Brian brushed his fingertips across her forehead. "I did, too."

He took a quick shower and changed into clean clothing. Gail hadn't stirred when he came back in. After snagging a bottle of water out of the refrigerator, he stretched out on the easy chair and propped his feet up on the ottoman.

He realized he'd never watched a woman sleep before. She lay on her side facing him, and he could see the complete relaxation in her body. A hint of sunburn toasted her nose and cheeks, and he'd swear there was a speck of barbecue sauce along the corner of her mouth.

He thought of the life nestled within her. The life they'd created.

"We can find a way to do this long-term, Gail," he murmured. "I believe it. I think in time you can believe it, too."

GAIL WASN'T SURE what happened. She felt a change blossoming deep inside her that wasn't all due to the baby. She liked having company during breakfast. Instead of reading the paper while bolting down her food, she found herself talking more. Brian was usually up earlier for his morning run and would have breakfast ready by the time she was up. He coaxed her into drinking herbal tea that she hated and drinking milk that she wasn't fond of, either.

She was forced to shorten her schedule at the office because mornings were still difficult for her. Brian insisted on driving her to and from the office the days he was off duty. She also found herself starting to take short naps in the afternoon. Normally, she would have fought what she would have considered his high-handedness, but she allowed it.

She also learned while Brian appeared easygoing, he could be just as stubborn as she was.

Because the day had been hot, Brian took his run in the evening. When he got back, he collapsed on a kitchen chair. A plastic bottle of orange juice sat near his hand.

"I don't see what satisfaction you get out of running," Gail said, coming into the kitchen. She was dressed in a lilac cotton robe with her hair pulled up in a short ponytail in deference to the still warm evening. Judging from the faint sheen of her skin and light fragrance in the air, she'd recently finished her bath.

"Keeps me in shape for work. You'd be surprised how many patients we have to haul down stairs. And some of them aren't lightweights." He slugged down another mouthful of juice. A towel lay wrapped around his neck. "But I give a group of high school girls a big charge when I run by." He grinned. "They're out there every night like clockwork."

Gail rolled her eyes. "They're probably wondering how an old guy can run like that without falling over." She snickered. She started rummaging through the cabinets.

"What're you looking for?"

"I'm hungry."

"What about dinner?"

"Oh sure, that mouthwatering egg white omelette and barely buttered toast you fixed me. Stuck to my ribs for all of three seconds." She slammed another cabinet door shut. "I thought we had some cookies."

Oh, boy. "The doctor said you had to watch your weight and sugar level, remember? You told me to take the cookies into the station, so you wouldn't be tempted."

An unladylike snarl left Gail's lips. She never had a problem with her weight until now. Then last week, John told her she was gaining weight too quickly and should be careful. Unfortunately, Brian was present and since then kept a close watch over her diet.

"Even a chocolate doughnut would be nice," she commented, turning around and leaning against the counter.

"Chocolate gives you heartburn," Brian reminded her.

"I'm willing to suffer." She sounded wistful. She braced her hands on the counter behind her. Soulful eyes studied him. "You have chocolate somewhere, don't you, Brian?"

"Nope." He drank more juice.

"Oh, Brian, you always have chocolate hidden," she murmured, keeping her gaze fastened on him. "You said you're not human without your daily chocolate fix. You know you're only hiding it because you think you're doing it for my own good. Except you're not. You're only making me suffer more."

His nerve endings tingled under the velvety caress of her voice. If she kept it up, he'd be tempted to carry her off somewhere and see what else he could get her to say. Such as, *Make love to me, Brian.*

He forced himself to sound nonchalant. "Not a good idea and you know it. Look what happened when you had that cup of hot chocolate a few nights ago. You were miserable."

"It was probably the milk. Dairy products can cause stomach upsets." She dipped her head and looked at him under the cover of her lashes. "I'm sure a doughnut wouldn't hurt me."

"And maybe it would." He had to be strong here. It was for her own good, he reminded himself. "You don't want to take that chance, Gail."

"I'll be fine. I only need to take some antacid afterward," she said softly.

"But why do it if you don't have to?" Brian felt frantic by now. He was weakening more by the second.

Gail arched her back. Her action caused her robe to stretch tightly across her breasts, which had grown fuller with her pregnancy. The soft cotton did nothing to hide the healthy curves.

He felt himself starting to dissolve.

"The doughnut shop is only a few blocks away. They're open twenty-four hours a day and have fresh doughnuts out every hour," she said in a voice he could only associate with the bedroom. "It wouldn't take long for you to run over there." Her lower lip stuck out in the faintest of pouts.

Hot damn! She was actually trying to seduce him. And all for a chocolate doughnut!

Brian felt his shorts tighten with his arousal. He resisted the urge to shift in his chair. He refused to allow himself to weaken. If he gave in over a doughnut, who knows what she'd demand next? She might go as far as to insist he get her a slice of double fudge cake or a hot fudge sundae!

He took a deep breath. "I've already cooled down. Not a good idea to take another run right now."

Gail's expression didn't change as she picked up her cup and plate and carried it over to the counter. Without saying a word, she headed down the hallway. Her hips swayed ever so slightly as she walked.

Brian heaved a silent sigh of relief. He was still reeling from this new side of Gail. If he hadn't seen it for himself, he wouldn't have believed she could act like a sly seductress just for a doughnut. A total departure from the slightly prim, buttoned-down Gail Roberts he was used to. He was grateful she dropped the subject instead of pursuing it. He was already on the verge of breaking down and racing down to the doughnut shop for a chocolate doughnut.

He continued sitting there enjoying the rest of his juice. Then the sound of a faint click had him shooting out of his chair as if someone had pulled the chair out from under him. He raced down the hallway, almost skidding to a stop in front of his bedroom doorway. He'd left the door open when he left his room that morning. Now it was closed. There was no mistaking the faint sounds of drawers opening and closing. And no mistaking who was doing it.

"Gail," he called out. "What are you doing?"

"I left some of my clothes in here," she called back. "Don't worry. I'll be out in a minute."

She couldn't come up with a better story than that? "You didn't leave any clothes in there."

"Oh, I'm sure I did."

He turned the knob, but it refused to move. She'd locked the door. "Come on, Gail, you don't need any chocolate."

"Then go down to the doughnut shop and buy me a chocolate doughnut!"

He winced at the strident sound in her voice.

Son, you're going to learn when a woman is pregnant and wants something you better get it or be prepared to suffer in ways you didn't believe were possible. Lou Walker's voice echoed in his head.

"You said it, Dad," he muttered, leaning against the wall.

The lock clicked and Gail walked out. She didn't look the least bit embarrassed or guilty. Instead, there was a hint of a self-satisfied smile on her face.

Brian closed his eyes in surrender.

"I better get ready for work," she murmured passing by him.

The faint scent of chocolate drifted along behind her.

Chapter Twelve

"It's just not fair! Why can't a person have some warning first?"

Gail's plaintive wail didn't sound good. Brian already was tired when he got up that morning. True to form, Gail was up most of last night suffering from a major attack of heartburn. He wanted to get up and see what he could do for her, but he sensed his life would have been in jeopardy if he had. Instead, he lay awake listening to her walk about the house. He visualized her taking antacid every time she could to calm the fire in her stomach. He wished he could have been with her, comforting her any way he could. But all he would have been was a reminder he told her what eating chocolate would do to her.

No, he wouldn't remind her he knew she suffered for eating those two candy bars she found in his nightstand.

As his dad would have told him, he was learning self-preservation the hard way.

But this he could do. He made his way down the hall and hovered inside her bedroom doorway.

Gail sat on the edge of her bed looking as forlorn as a puppy. Piles of clothes surrounded her and fell over onto the floor. All she wore was a light green thin cotton camisole that stretched tightly over her rounded belly and matching panties that seemed to have trouble staying up. It was as if she'd suddenly turned into an earthy woman overnight.

Brian tamped down the instant lust that rose up at the lush sight before him. He wasn't too sure she'd like it that he wanted to push aside all the clothing and have his way with her.

Obviously, all his running wasn't helping curb his libido one bit.

"Considering what I'm seeing there, I can't imagine you're going to tell me you don't have anything to wear," he said lightly.

Wrong words. He knew it the second she looked up at him.

"Nothing fits," she said mournfully, picking up a pair of taupe linen pants and putting them back down. "Oh, they didn't fit very well before, but I was doing all right. All of a sudden my blouses are too snug and my pants won't even come near what used to be my waist."

Brian didn't waste any time in going over to her. He crouched down in front of her and took her hands in his.

"The kid isn't cooperating, huh?" He rubbed her hands with his fingers. "I know I'm a man and wouldn't know anything about these secret women things you're going through right now. And while the worst thing I can do is say anything about a woman's weight," he winced at the glare she directed at him, "I do have to remind you that you are pregnant. Maybe it's time to do some shopping for maternity clothes." A groan sounded inside him. He always equated shopping with having a root canal.

"I just need something in a larger size," she murmured. "No more fitted waistbands. Everything comfortable."

"Okay. We'll go shopping today." That mournful internal groan sounded again.

Her lashes sparkled with tears. "Nothing fits," she whispered. "I can't get into anything now."

Brian nodded. "No prob." He straightened up and grabbed her cordless phone. He left the room as he made the call. When he came back in, he was smiling. "Go take your shower and do whatever else that will make you feel better. Everything will be fine." He grasped her hands and pulled her upright. He sent her on her way with a pat on her butt. She glared at him over her shoulder, but it didn't have the power it usually would have.

Brian waited by the front window watching. The moment a red Explorer pulled into the driveway, he had the front door open and waited for the woman to walk up.

"Hey, hot stuff." He kissed Abby on the cheek. "You're rescuing her and me."

She held up a large handled shopping bag. "I've been there and I know the feeling."

"Abby?" Dressed in a robe, Gail walked out into the living room.

"Hi, Gail. I understand you reached what you feel is the point of no return," Abby told her. "When I was carrying the twins I swore I blew up twenty-five pounds overnight. Brian said he's offered to take you clothes shopping today, which is incredible since the Walker men aren't known for their patience in malls. I brought a couple things over for you to wear. And if you'd rather not go along with this guy here," she sent Brian a sly smile, "I'm volunteering."

Gail reluctantly took the bag. "You must have things to do."

Abby shook her head. "Things more important than shopping? I don't think so! Jeff's watching the girls and I need to pick up some things anyway." She turned Gail around and gave her a gentle shove. "Go on. We'll spend the day with our charge cards."

"All right." Gail glanced at Brian. "You don't mind?"

"I could go with the two of you," he offered. "Carry packages. That kind of thing."

"I'm sure you can find something useful to do while we have a girl's day out," Abby told him.

Brian looked at Gail. "Rumor has it she can bring a mall to its knees in no time," he said. "Think you can handle that?"

"Since I don't shop very much, this could prove informative."

He went over to Gail and wrapped his hands around her arms. She still held the bag Abby brought her.

"Go change and have some fun," he whispered for her ears only. "I guess Abby can show you a kind of fun I can't."

She looked past him toward Abby. "Give me ten minutes."

"I'm in no hurry. This way I can snoop." Abby waited until Gail disappeared down the hallway. "How's she doing otherwise?"

"She still has the nausea and there's times when she's so stubborn about something you'd think her spine would snap from all the steel," he replied.

Abby reached up and took his face between her hands. She peered closely into his eyes. "And what about you? Are you doing this just because you're a nice guy?"

"There's something about her, Abby," he admitted. "You know, she's a hotshot doctor, lives what seems the good life, but there's still something missing there. I guess I'm here to find out what it is."

Abby patted his cheek. "Oh yes, you are and you will," she said mysteriously.

Before Brian could question her further, Gail returned wearing dark blue knit shorts and a blue print T-shirt that was full enough to flow over her rounded tummy.

"Definitely a better color for you than me," Abby pronounced. "A day of shopping will have you feeling like your old self in no time. I know it helps me." She opened the front door. "We'll also go for a blow out lunch. That's what I love about being pregnant. No guilt on eating."

"She has heartburn if she eats chocolate," Brian warned. "And the doctor said she has to watch what she eats because she's gaining weight too fast."

"Thank you, Dr. Walker, for that insightful update," Gail grumbled, giving him a quick kick in the ankle.

Abby made a face. "As if that stops us. I get heartburn every time I eat ice cream. Jeff will tell you that doesn't stop me from eating it. You just let us worry about our stomachs, okay?" She waved over her shoulder as she left.

"I should be angry with you for calling Abby about my problem, but I guess I can't." Gail stood up on her toes and kissed him.

What should have started out as a light kiss quickly moved into more as Brian put his arms around her and drew her closer.

"Excuse me! You two can think about doing that later! The stores are open and calling our names!" Abby shouted. "As for you, Walker, get a hobby!"

Gail stepped back and looked at Brian. Startled awareness shone brightly in her eyes and a faint pink colored her cheeks that traveled down her throat. Her lips were moist and slightly parted. She had to be aware she had made the first move. Something she hadn't really done before. He thought about kicking the door shut in Abby's face and carrying Gail back to bed.

Damn! He was thinking about that way too much. There've been too many nights they shared a house but not a bed. Every day, he thought about a repeat of that magical night. But he took it slow because he didn't want to scare her off. Maybe he should think about speeding up his plan.

Gail took several steps backward. "I'll see you later," she murmured.

"Yeah." He still found it hard to breathe. He raised his voice. "Hey, Abby. Take care of my little one."

THE DAY turned into an education for Gail. Before, she'd only shopped for clothing when she absolutely had to. And then, she usually called a personal shopper at her favorite department store and let the consultant pick out a selection of clothing for her to choose from.

Not with Abby. Abby attacked stores the way Sherman marched through Georgia. She searched maternity departments along with others with a single mindedness that rivaled Gail's.

"Anything with an elastic waistband is good," she told Gail, tossing a couple of skirts over her arm along with a long denim jumper. "Tops a couple sizes too big. Sometimes you can go that route for your entire pregnancy. Sometimes you have no choice but to wear maternity clothes if you don't want to feel constricted. When I was pregnant with the girls I was excited to wear maternity clothes. By the end of my pregnancy, I hated everything in my closet.'' She added some brightly colored T-shirts to the pile. She grabbed one off the rack, held it up then handed it to Gail. ''This would look great on you. Good for when you're working.''

''I usually wear something more classic,'' she murmured, eyeing the bold fuchsia shirt with a wary eye.

Abby stopped and turned around. ''I may well warn you now. Until the child is twenty-one, you might as well forget wearing clothing that is dry-clean only. Forget silk, rayon, anything that requires special care. From now on, think easy maintenance. Wash-and-wear clothing and wash and wear hair. There will be no such thing as a schedule because babies have their own schedule that will never mesh with your own.''

''I have babies spit up on me all the time,'' Gail explained.

''Do you intend to wear a lab coat or scrubs until the baby grows up? Because that's what you'd have to do. It never fails to happen when you least expect it. I ruined three of my favorite outfits before I got smart. I even started wearing some of Jeff's old shirts.'' She moved on, pulled out a turquoise sleeveless dress and added it to Gail's armload.

''I don't know if that color would look good on me,'' Gail murmured.

''It should. You have the coloring for it.'' Abby cocked her head to one side, studying Gail from head to foot. ''It's time you thought about a big change.''

She looked at the pile of clothing in her arms. All styles and colors she never considered before. ''I think I already have.''

By the time the day was over, Gail had a brand-new wardrobe that left her feeling comfortable and would work for her for the rest of her pregnancy. Not stopping there, Abby talked her into flats and sandals and even new makeup in bolder colors to go with her new clothes.

When Gail saw the red dress she'd bought for the dinner but ended up ruined, she couldn't help but purchase another one.

"Why Gail, you are a wild one after all." Abby grinned, examining the sexy dress.

"Let's just say the dress changed my life in more ways than I'd like to count."

With Abby, Gail found someone who understood what she was going through. She could also give her insight into Brian. Insight that might help Gail understand what was happening to her emotions just now where he was concerned.

"From what I've heard, everyone thought Brian would marry first. He loves kids, has always talked about having some of his own and seems to have the perfect family-man mentality," Abby told her over lunch. "The girls love him to pieces. In fact, all his nephews and nieces do."

Gail toyed with her salad. "He says children understand him because he never grew up."

"That's true." She chucked. "He is one big kid himself. No one can help but love him." She studied Gail for so long the other woman shifted uneasily under her gaze. "You are so different than any of the women he's dated. Not that it's been all that many."

"I knew we were too different the first time we met."

"Sometimes, those differences make it better. You and Brian can balance each other."

"He's only staying with me because he seems to think I can't take care of myself," she argued.

Abby shook her head. "You're afraid of something

more, aren't you? And don't say you're not," she added.
"I've been there. It's easier to fight if you believe it.
Other than Jeff, you will never have better dad material
than Brian. I don't think you're the type of woman who
would make love with a man unless there was something
there. Maybe you need to give Brian and yourself a
chance to see just what is there between you other than
a baby."

"So tell me, Dr. Walker, do you give this pep talk to
all of your brother-in-law's women?" Gail asked.

"Are you kidding?" She laughed. "You're the first
one I've actually liked. Not that he chooses duds or
twits. But I could see they didn't appreciate Brian for
who he is. Which is a real sweetheart."

"I guess you could say I appreciate the fact he's as
stubborn as a mule," she pointed out.

"Then you're halfway there."

Abby's words stuck with Gail for the rest of the day.

She was leery of kissing Brian or touching him because of the way it made her feel. Although, she noticed
he always found an excuse to put his arms around her
to give her a hug or drop a kiss on her forehead or lips.
Usually the latter. For someone unused to such open
signs of affection, she was growing addicted to his
touch.

Today had been the first time she made the first move.
She surprised herself. Even more surprising was her
stronger-than-usual reaction to the kiss. She could try to
blame it on hormones, but she knew doing so would
only brand her a liar.

By the time Abby returned Gail home, her charge
cards had been used heavily, and most of the packages
in the back of the truck were hers. Not only had she
treated herself to a new wardrobe, but she also picked

up things for the baby that she found irrestible. She should have been panicking over spending as much as she had. She'd always been careful with her money before. A habit she'd learned from her parents. Instead, the spending spree left her exhilarated.

"I always felt the most fun was putting everything away," Abby told her, as she helped her carry bags into the house. "Sort of like Christmas."

"When the bills arrive next month I'll probably tell myself to completely forget about Christmas this year," Gail said dryly. She halted when an unfamiliar sound came from the backyard. She would have worried if she hadn't then heard Brian's voice. "What is that?" She laid the packages on the couch and headed for the rear of the house with Abby following her.

The sight in the backyard was more than Gail expected. Brian, wearing only a pair of faded black cotton shorts, was running around the backyard with a black-and-tan puppy happily running after him.

"Come on, boy, let's go for it," he urged the puppy.

"Congratulations, Gail, it looks like you're a mother already." Abby slid open the screen door. "Don't tell us. He followed you home, right?"

Brian looked up and grinned. "Dad called and said Lady Jane's puppies were old enough to leave their mom. And we could have one as an early baby gift," he told them. The puppy followed close on his heels. "I went over there, and this guy came right up to me."

"If Lou called Jeff with the same story, I will kill him," Abby moaned.

"Jeff and the girls were over there," Brian admitted. "But that doesn't mean they went home with a puppy."

"Oh sure they didn't. The girls have been begging for a dog since they saw the last Lassie movie. Maybe

I better hope that they didn't take two home." Abby crouched down and scratched the puppy's head. The dog sat there looking blissful under her touch. "He is cute, but not when the girls aren't old enough to take care of themselves, much less a dog."

"German shepherds are excellent watchdogs," Brian told her. "They're also great with kids. Look how great Lady Jane is."

"And they eat like horses." Abby heaved a sigh. "I guess I better head home and see what they came home with." She turned and hugged Gail. "Let him do all the cleaning up," she said loud enough for Brian to hear. "Speaking as one who knows, you two are perfect for each other," she whispered. "I'll call you later."

Gail couldn't stop looking at the puppy who calmly squatted and peed all over the concrete. She could feel the dismay take over. She felt as helpless about pets as she did her upcoming baby.

"Obviously, he's not housebroken. "

Brian hunkered down and praised the puppy. "At least he wasn't in the house. He already seems to understand he's supposed to go outside and not inside." He held out his hand. "Come on, make friends with him. I haven't named him yet. I thought we should do it together."

She looked indecisive. "You've had dogs before."

"Dogs, cats, guinea pigs, hamsters, even a boa constrictor once," he replied. As he kept looking up at her, her actions finally dawned on him. "You've never had a pet before, have you?"

"My father was allergic to animal fur. At least, that was my parents' excuse." She slowly bent down and held out her hand. The puppy, sensing a new audience, immediately swiped his tongue across her palm. Startled, she started to draw back, but Brian grabbed her wrist and held it still.

"He just wants to get to know you," he explained softly.

The puppy then sniffed every inch of her hand and arm. Deciding Gail was acceptable, his jaw opened in a wide yawn and he plopped down.

"Brian—" she was interrupted before she could say anymore.

"I know. I should have talked about this with you," he admitted. "I went over there and the minute he looked up at me, I knew he was perfect for the baby. They can grow up together."

"They chew things," she said helplessly. "And make messes. And bark all night. And shed. And he'll have to be fixed so we don't end up with dog paternity suits all over the neighborhood." She thought of her neighbor's championship poodle and shuddered.

"German shepherds have shorter fur. You train them not to chew or make messes," he said logically. "He'll only bark for a good reason or if he's playing. As for the surgery," he said reluctantly, "you have to wait until they're at least six months old."

To ease the ache in her thighs, Gail kneeled down on the patio. The puppy, obviously tired from all his play, now lay on his side, panting softly. To her, he looked like an adorable stuffed animal a child would enjoy holding during the night. Except she knew this one wasn't found at a toy store. The puppy was no fool. He lifted his head and sensed the nice-smelling lady was weakening. He made his way over to her and plopped himself into her lap. He laid his head across her leg and promptly went to sleep. His body grew heavy as he twitched and whimpered puppy dreams.

She tentatively stroked his body, finding his fur soft to the touch. He opened one eye and swiped her hand with his tongue again.

Just as Gail had succumbed to bedroom-blue eyes, she now gave in to a pair of dark-brown eyes.

"Just as long as he isn't called Rover," she murmured her surrender.

Brian settled in next to her and put his arm around her. "Congratulations, Doc. You're a puppy mom."

"He chews one thing that's not his or makes one mess on the carpet and you're both out of here," she threatened, but there was no heat in her words. She knew it. And Brian knew it.

He held up his hand as he vowed, "He'll be fine, you'll see."

BRIAN'S PROMISE only lasted until that night. The puppy, now dubbed Duffy, was settled down in the laundry room in a basket filled with an old blanket and a ticking clock. His whimpers were soft at first then grew in crescendo as he realized no one was moving fast enough to rescue him.

"Come on, Duffy," Brian groaned, staggering out to the room. The puppy sat up and wagged his tail. He whimpered and stumbled out of the basket.

"What's wrong?" Gail appeared behind him. She hid a yawn behind her hand as she leaned against a counter.

"I don't think he accepts the clock as a substitute for his mom," he replied, squatting down as the puppy ambled over to him and tried to climb into his lap.

"What can we do?" It didn't take her long to figure it out. "That dog is not sleeping in the bed!"

"It's his first night away from his brothers and sis-

ters.'' He stood up with the puppy cradled in his arms.
"He needs reassurance.''

"How are you expected to be firm with him if you
give in to him the first time he cries?'' she asked.

"Just for tonight.''

She spun around and walked away. "I can see who
will discipline the baby.''

A half hour later, Gail was just drifting off to sleep
when she heard a faint sound by her bed. She rose up
on her elbow and looked over the side of the bed. She
didn't expect to see Duffy sitting there, his head cocked
to one side. Tiny whimpers left his throat. By all rights,
she should take him back to the laundry room so he
would learn that was where he should sleep every night.
Even if he would start crying and howling again.

"If my mother knew I was doing this, she would have
a stroke,'' she whispered, reaching down and picking
the puppy up.

As if he'd always done it, Duffy circled several times
before he settled in the middle of the covers on the other
side of the bed. A huge sigh left his body as he fell
asleep.

Gail lay on her side, watching the puppy sleep peacefully now that he was where he wanted to be.

"You and Brian are making sure my life will never
be the same,'' she whispered, stretching out one hand
so that her fingers rested against the puppy's fur.

When Brian went in search of Duffy the next morning, he feared he'd find chewed furniture or even worse.
He didn't expect to find the puppy sleeping on Gail's
bed with her curled up beside him, her hand resting on
the puppy's side. When he quietly entered the room, the
puppy looked up and gave him a lopsided puppy grin.

"I don't blame you for wanting to stay, fella. But I

think she'd prefer it that you go outside and do your business before you have an accident,'' Brian whispered, carefully picking up the puppy and draping him over his shoulder. "Think if I whimper and look pathetic she'll let me stay in here too?"

Chapter Thirteen

"Dr. Gail, why'd you want to have a baby?" Adam asked Gail. "They're really noisy and messy." He wiggled on the examination table with typical little boy impatience. "My baby sister cries all the time. And she smells awful bad." He wrinkled his nose.

"Adam!" His mother frowned at him.

Gail chuckled. "I hate to tell you this, Adam, but once upon a time you were a baby," she told him.

"We didn't sleep for more than two hours at a time for the first six months," his mother said. "But I guess as a doctor you're used to sleeping in snatches from your intern days."

Gail nodded as she wrote in Adam's chart. "There's some redness in his throat and I'll swab for strep, just in case. His temperature was normal and his glands are only slightly swollen. I'm going to prescribe some antibiotics."

"Ones that will keep him drowsy will be fine with me," the woman murmured.

Gail grinned. "I'll see what I can do."

"Then I promise the kids won't get sick while you're gone on maternity leave." She took the prescription. "Do yourself a favor and have a girl."

After they left, Gail sat back in her chair. Her back seemed to be aching more each day.

She was discovering that her patients' parents had been wonderful about her pregnancy. Admittedly, unwed motherhood was nothing new, but there would always be a few who wouldn't appreciate their children being treated by an unwed mother. Instead, Gail received advice right and left and one little girl even drew a picture she said was for the baby's nursery. Touched, Gail put it away with the intention of having it framed and hung.

"Dr. Roberts?" Lora stuck her head around the door. "The hair salon just called and said Holly went home sick. They asked if you want to reschedule."

Gail thought of her hair, which had been giving her fits lately. "Do me a favor and ask if Ginna is free any time this afternoon," she asked. "I'll take any opening she has."

"Will do." She disappeared. A couple of minutes later she returned. "Ginna can take you at the same time you were scheduled with Holly."

"Thank you, Lora." She slowly stood up.

"You okay?" the receptionist asked.

"Just feeling a bit off balance," she explained.

She had just returned to her office when Sheila walked in.

"You don't have anyone else," Sheila announced, setting a glass of sparkling mineral water on the desktop, "so you can finish charts before you go for your hair appointment."

"Oh, gee," Gail drawled. "You're so good to me." She picked up the glass.

"How ya feeling?" Sheila sat down across from her.

"Like I'm carrying a bowling ball." She expelled a deep sigh. "I hate to think what I'll feel like in a few months."

"Probably like you're carrying two bowling balls. Tall, dark and handsome picking you up when you're finished?"

Gail shook her head. "He's on duty."

"It must be lonely when he's not around."

"I've got Duffy." She thought of the puppy who seemed to grow more each day. And who slept each night on her bed. The puppy seemed to sense he wasn't welcome until after Brian went to bed. Then he would creep into the bedroom and she would lift him onto her bed. She always made sure to get up early so she could put him back in his own bed before Brian got up.

She wouldn't admit it to anyone, but the puppy's presence each night was comforting.

"How often does Brian call to check up on you?"

"Every chance he can," Gail said. "Abby said the men are giving him a hard time for being such a worrier."

"Most prospective fathers are that way," Sheila told her. "You're lucky."

"He plans to paint the nursery his next few days off. We're going shopping for furniture next week." She couldn't stop the warmth that flowed through her.

Brian was making it more and more difficult to resist him. And damn him, he had to know it! She'd read that a pregnant woman's libido increased, and she knew hers had done so tenfold.

The way she was thinking, it was a good thing he was on duty. She might have gone home and pounced on him! She quickly finished her water hoping the cold liquid would cool her off in time.

GAIL ALWAYS enjoyed her visits to Steppin' Out's salon and spa. She found it the one place where she felt she could truly relax. Except now she kept eyes forward when she walked past the Blind Date Central board.

A local magazine described the salon's interior as hip with its black-and-white tile floor, black marbleized counters and 1940s swing music playing in the background. Even the stylists wore only black and white to keep with the theme. Double glass doors in the rear stood open as an invitation to enter the day spa where the ambience was the exact opposite. There, relaxation was the key. A woman bubbling over with enthusiasm was explaining to the receptionist it was her birthday. Gail guessed she was there for the first time.

Ginna approached Gail looking elegant in an ankle-length black skirt and white silk wrap top. Her dark hair was piled on top of her head in a mass of curls.

"You look good," she greeted her.

Gail looked down at the denim jumper and soft pink T-shirt she wore. Not at all what she was used to, but she had to admit she looked good in it.

"It was time for something that would fit," she said as Ginna settled her in the leather chair.

"Haircut time?" Ginna ran her fingers through Gail's hair.

"Something low maintenance," she remembered Abby's advice.

"How about something shorter that you can pretty much wash and wear?" Ginna suggested.

"Sounds good to me."

Ginna kept up easy talk while she trimmed Gail's hair.

"It's only the men in the family who are demented,"

she told Gail. "Luckily, the women always turned out normal."

"Which is why I ended up with a puppy?" she said dryly.

"You won't regret it. A built-in playmate for the baby, and Lady Jane does have wonderful puppies. I have one from her previous litter who's a dream. Casper's great company and even better protection when I go running."

"Another runner."

Ginna laughed at Gail's groan. "Mom started us running. When we were little we'd go for hikes in the hills. The running just grew out of it. Dad preferred staying home. His idea of exercise is walking to the refrigerator." She picked up her round brush and switched on the hair dryer. "You'll find this style very easy to manage."

When she finished, Gail found herself with hair just below her ears and parted on the side. Ginna brushed it out and tucked it behind her ears.

The style was more easygoing than Gail was used to wearing. But it went with her outfit.

I am definitely changing, she thought to herself as she viewed her reflection in the mirror.

"I really like it." She smiled at the woman.

"If I thought I could be lucky with the blind date board, I'd give it a try myself," Ginna said lightly before hugging Gail. "I'm glad to see you again."

"And I'm glad I asked for you." She hugged her back.

Listening to her stomach, Gail picked up her favorite Chinese takeout before driving home.

"It's orange chicken for us, baby," she said out loud. "And fried rice and steamed vegetables."

Once home, she put a whimpering Duffy outside then spooned her food onto a plate. She carried it outside and sat at the patio table while Duffy wandered around the yard.

Normally, she would have enjoyed her favorite food. But since Brian had moved in, she found the times she was alone not as peaceful as she used to. She missed his free and easy banter. Missed watching him run around the yard with Duffy.

Basically, she just plain missed him.

She picked up her fortune cookie and broke it open. In the fading light she could still read the typed words. *All you require is by your side.*

Gail looked down at Duffy who lay sprawled by her feet. His eyes were closed and his legs twitching as he dreamed.

"I never did like their fortunes." She gently rubbed her tummy.

"C'MON, DUFFY, I know you can do it." Brian tossed the ball a short distance away then ran to it to show the dog what he meant.

Gail laughed as she watched the puppy sit there, his tongue lolling and the expression on his face saying, *Is he funny or what?*

"I think Duffy would prefer watching you." She carefully sat down on the grass. She stretched her legs out in front of her, enjoying the feel of the cool grass against her bare legs. The full skirt of her turquoise dress was mashed down when Duffy hopped into her lap. He barked several times and bounced up to lick her face.

"Augh! Duffy!" she shrieked, laughing at the same time.

Knowing she wasn't angry with him, the puppy kept

leaping up until Gail fell back with the dog sprawled on her chest.

"Hey, how come I'm not in on this?" Brian sat down behind her, angling his legs alongside hers. She laughed when he stroked her tummy. "This kid is really starting to kick. I told you. A boy."

"Girl," she argued, still laughing as she leaned back against his chest.

"Gail?"

Gail froze at the sound of the shocked voice. She turned her head and saw her parents standing just outside the patio door. It might have been Saturday, but her father was dressed in suit and tie as if he'd just left the office. Her mother's linen dress didn't dare show one wrinkle.

"We rang the bell," her father said in his correct tone. "Did you realize your front door was unlocked? That's not very safe."

"Definitely not safe," her mother echoed.

Both sets of eyes fastened on Brian. The expressions on their faces said it all.

Gail knew what they saw. Brian had told her she didn't need a gardening service, so he mowed the front yard and trimmed the shrubs early in the day. He was still in stained khaki shorts and running shoes that were worse for wear. His tanned chest was sweaty and bare with dirt and leaves on his damp skin.

"Did you happen to hurt yourself, and your gardener is assisting you?" Irene Roberts asked. She looked at Duffy as if he were a monster in miniature. "And his dog?"

Gail realized with the position she was in, her pregnancy wasn't apparent. She suddenly wished she'd told them earlier.

"Mother, Father, this is Brian Walker," she said, putting Duffy to one side and starting to get to her feet. Brian immediately went to her side and gave her a hand up. "Brian, these are my parents, Irene and Patrick Walker."

"I'm very pleased to meet you." Brian held out his hand.

Patrick looked as if he wanted to ignore the outstretched hand, but good manners won out.

It was then the two older people got a good look at Gail.

Patrick's eyebrows rose up to meet his hairline. Irene gasped. Patrick looked from Gail to Brian.

"I gather he is the father." The older man's voice could have frozen hell.

Gail felt the encouraging warmth of Brian's hand covering hers. "Yes, he is."

"I guess I should be grateful you didn't get pregnant during medical school or your internship when it would have completely derailed your work," Patrick said.

"Why didn't you tell us?" Irene demanded. She made her way over to the patio table. She brushed off the chair surface before seating herself. "How could you let us find out this way?"

"I thought all you cared about was your career," Patrick said, giving Brian a less than friendly look. "What does he do?"

"Why don't you ask Brian that question," Gail said sharply. "He's very fluent in English."

"What did you do to your hair?" Irene asked, frowning at Gail's tousled style. She had her hair pulled back with a turquoise hairband today.

"It's called low-maintenance hair," she explained. "Much better to keep up once the baby comes."

"I can't imagine why you chose such a strong color." Irene's frown continued its way down to her dress.

"It's bright and cheerful. And I like it." Gail wasn't backing down.

"So, what do you do?" Patrick turned his forceful glare on Brian.

"I'm a paramedic with the county fire department, sir," Brian replied.

"Flunked out of medical school?"

Gail winced, but Brian proved he could handle himself.

"I'd rather be down there in the trenches than wearing a fancy white coat," he explained. "We also do a lot of rescue work."

"How could you get a dog?" Irene stared at Duffy as if he were something covered with fleas. She reared back when the puppy ambled in her direction.

"Actually, Duffy's still a puppy," Gail said, taking the chair next to her mother's. She was no longer worried about Brian. He could clearly hold his own with her father.

"But they pick up parasites. Make such horrible messes."

"Now that you've gotten my daughter pregnant, don't you think you'd do her a larger favor by getting out of her life?" Patrick boomed. "A great deal of money was spent on her education. I don't intend to see it go to waste because of this lapse in her life."

"Father!" Gail stood up so suddenly, she had to grasp the patio table to keep her balance. "That was uncalled for."

Brian didn't take his eyes from Patrick's face. "It's okay, Gail. I'm just waiting for your old man to offer me money to leave you alone. Then he'll talk to you about putting the baby up for adoption since he can't imagine you would want to be saddled with some low-life's kid.''

"Children put such a cramp in one's life," Irene said, unthinking how much her careless words would hurt her daughter.

"Yes, I'm sure they do," Gail said, tight-lipped. She swallowed a groan when the patio door opened again. Her features relaxed when Cathy, Lou, Theo and a silver-haired woman stepped outside.

"Hello, dear, I brought over a coconut cake," Cathy greeted Gail. Either she was oblivious to the tension in the air or ignoring it. She walked over to Gail and hugged her. "I hope we didn't interrupt anything."

Gail saw the twinkle in her eye and knew Cathy had figured out things were not going well.

"Cathy, Lou, Theo—" She looked at the woman standing next to the elderly man.

"I'm Martha, dear." She smiled.

"And Martha." She smiled back. "My parents, Patrick and Irene Roberts. Mother, Father, these are Brian's parents and grandparents."

"Pleased to meet you." Lou held out his hand.

Theo merely glowered and nodded.

Patrick glanced around. "You didn't sign over any of your investments to him, did you?"

That was it.

Gail might have been in a flowing dress and barefoot, but when necessary she carried herself with her father's rigid demeanor. Right now, it was necessary.

"These people have showed me more concern and affection in a few months than you did my entire life," she said in a low voice. "I want my baby to know his or her grandparents. If you want to be a part of that life, fine. If not, then I truly feel sorry for you.''

''Irene.'' Patrick didn't take his eyes off his daughter.

Irene stood up and walked over to her husband.

''We gave up a lot for you,'' he told Gail.

She didn't back down. ''Not what counts.''

She stood there and watched them leave. She didn't move when Brian's hands rested on her shoulders.

''Are you all right?'' he asked, his lips close to her ear.

Not trusting her voice, she settled for a brief nod.

''Oh, my dear.'' Cathy gently pushed Brian to one side and gathered Gail in her arms.

''Are you sure you weren't raised by robots?'' Theo boomed. ''Because they sure couldn't have been human.''

''Theo!'' Martha scolded, slapping at her husband's arm.

''I've seen a car with more emotion,'' he grumbled.

Cathy kept her hold on Gail and looked over Gail's shoulder toward her son. ''Why don't you bring out the cake I brought.''

''I better do it. They'll steal bites while slicing it.'' Martha turned toward the door.

''I'll show you where everything is, Gram.'' Brian went with her.

''Hey, fella,'' Lou coaxed the puppy onto the lawn. Theo followed.

''I don't cry,'' Gail whispered against Cathy's shoulder.

''Of course not, dear,'' the older woman said soothingly. ''Had they known about the pregnancy?''

''Not until ten minutes ago. It never seemed a good time to tell them.''

"Then give them time to let it settle in and sit down and have a talk with them."

"That's not the way my father works," Gail said. "My own mother admitted children were a hindrance."

"Then she didn't realize what a joy they are. Although, I admit more of a fondness for grandchildren," Cathy murmured. "I spoil them and send them home to their parents."

"I'm so glad my baby will have you!" she cried, holding on to her tightly.

"And I'm glad my son has you," she told her. "Just put him out of his misery and realize exactly what you have." She looked up. "Here they are!"

Cathy took charge, sending the men to eat their cake on the lawn while the women sat at the table. While they sat there, Martha presented Gail with a shawl she'd knitted for her. Gail exclaimed over the soft lilac color and marveled how soft it was. She kept it in her lap unable to stop stroking the fabric.

"Maybe it's old-fashioned, but I always felt a new mother should have a shawl to wear when she's up nights with the baby," the older woman smiled. "Men tend to sleep through those hours."

"Lou found it hard to sleep through them when I'd thump him awake." Cathy chuckled.

"Theo said you stood up to him," Martha said to Gail. "Any woman who can do that is made for this family."

"I thought it was more my being a pediatrician that helped deal with them." Gail ate a bite of cake and closed her eyes in bliss. "This is fantastic."

"I usually make a chocolate cake with coconut filling and frosting but with chocolate giving you heartburn, I made a white cake instead," Cathy explained.

Gail felt twinges that her parents couldn't accept Brian and his family. She remembered Cathy talking about the news apparently being a shock. She made a vow to call her mother later in the week. She feared she already knew the answer, but she'd give it a try.

As she ate her cake, she looked over at Brian who sat on the grass with his father and grandfather. Duffy bounced from one to the other looking for crumbs. Sensing her gaze on him, he looked at her and winked.

Gail felt something she'd never experienced before. Whatever barriers she'd erected against Brian before had completely fallen down.

She'd feared a relationship because she didn't want the cold uncaring union her parents shared.

From the beginning, Brian showed he was anything but cold and uncaring. They were opposites, but they managed to balance each other. She was glad she realized it before it was too late.

BRIAN FIRST sensed it as a shift in the air. It began when his parents and grandparents were there. Nothing more than a look Gail gave him. A hint of smile when she passed by him.

The piece of cake turned into their staying for dinner. Brian barbecued with help from his dad and granddad who actually argued over how to do it properly.

He was glad they'd shown up when they did. Gail's parents had upset her, and he hated to think what the rest of the day would have been like for her if she'd had to think about their visit. He wasn't sure what his mom said to Gail, but it must have been good.

"I really like your grandmother," Gail said, as she curled up in the easy chair. She'd showered and changed into her nightgown. The soft coral cotton fabric draped down to her ankles as she sat back.

Brian noticed since her shopping trip with Abby that Gail wore brighter colors that turned out to be rich accents to her dark coloring. That she was comfortable enough around him to not bother with a robe said a lot to him. Except right now, the way the material stretched over her breasts and molded her belly, she might have been safer wearing a robe. No, he'd rather sit back and enjoy the view.

"Yeah, Gram is the best," he admitted. He sat on the couch and stretched his legs out.

"You are so lucky to have them." She leaned over and picked up Duffy who'd been clamoring to climb up. The puppy circled several times and plopped down in her lap.

Brian eyed the puppy with envy.

"Your own parents just need to get used to the idea of becoming grandparents."

Gail shook her head. "They'll never get used to it. They didn't get used to being parents." She stroked Duffy's back. "That's all right." She smiled at Brian.

He felt his stomach lurch. Oh, she smiled at him all the time, but he noticed a lot of extra wattage this time.

"It is?"

She nodded. "The baby will have us and have your family. Isn't that what counts? Especially when they'll have you for a father."

Brian got to his feet and walked over to Gail. He sat down on the ottoman, picking up her feet and placing them in his lap. He treated her to a foot massage. Duffy opened one eye. Realizing his spot was still safe, he went back to snoozing.

"You knew your parents would react the way they

did, didn't you?'' he commented. "That's why you weren't all that eager in telling them.''

She kept her attention focused on the puppy as she kept stroking his fur. "They don't like anything that interferes with their lives.''

"I think I know what happened. Babies were switched at the hospital.'' He moved her forward far enough that he could slide in behind her. He settled her back against him with his arms around her. She snuggled in closer. "There's some sweet couple out there who can't understand why their daughter acts as if she has a computer chip for a heart.'' He rested his chin on her shoulder.

Her shoulders shook with her laughter.

"She doesn't smile. She doesn't laugh. Doesn't think pets are a good idea and dust doesn't dare settle in her house,'' he added. "Maybe she teaches at a military academy. She'd be perfect there.''

"Stop it!'' she pleaded, still laughing.

"Or maybe she's a judge. Not a lawyer. She'd have to be a judge because she'd want to dispense punishment.''

Gail twisted around in his lap. "You are terrible,'' she choked.

"I'm just pointing out what happened. I bet a DNA test would prove me right,'' he said straight-faced.

"Stop now,'' she ordered without heat.

"I know how to draw blood,'' he offered.

"Brian!''

He pulled her closer.

Gail didn't stop to think. She leaned in and kissed him.

"Brian," she whispered, drawing back. "I should have been kissing you more."

"We can make up for lost time," he whispered back.

Her smile was megawatt. "I think that's an excellent idea."

Chapter Fourteen

Gail couldn't remember ever just sitting there, cuddling with and kissing a man.

"I should have done this more often," she murmured. "It's nice."

"Of course, it's nice," he murmured back, nibbling on her ear. "More than nice. There's nothing like spending the evening in a hot-and-heavy make-out session. Especially when there's no parents around to interrupt."

She turned her head in his direction, purring under his attention. She traced the colorful design on his T-shirt.

"Your shark is fading," she whispered as his lips glided over hers.

"Sharks don't fade away, they just head for deeper waters." His hands rested lightly on her burgeoning belly. "Does he do this all the time?" He referred to the rolling motions under his palms.

"*She's* dancing." She slid her hands upward against his hot skin. His nipples were like tiny pebbles under her fingertips. She shifted on his lap, feeling the hard ridge of his arousal under her.

Brian suddenly lurched forward. He grabbed Duffy and set him down on the floor. The puppy momentarily whimpered then wandered off in search of something to play with.

"It's not raining, Gail," Brian said in a tight voice.

She smiled. "No, it's not."

"We're not in a stranger's house and there's no fire burning."

Gail shifted again in his lap. "Oh, I think there's a fire burning somewhere."

Brian put her to one side and stood up. Before she could ask him what he was doing, he picked her up in his arms.

"I'm too heavy," she protested, looping her arms around his neck.

He grimaced and pretended to stagger. "Wow, you're right," he groaned theatrically. "I hope I don't throw out my back."

"Brian!"

He kissed her quickly. "No more games," he told her, his meaning clear. He lifted her higher in his arms and walked down the hallway. He didn't stop until they reached her bedroom. There, he placed her on the bed as carefully as if she were a delicate figurine.

Gail scooted over so that Brian could follow her down.

"I've been dreaming about this every night," he told her, pulling her back into his arms.

"You never did anything about it." Her words said even more. That she wished he'd followed up on his feelings.

"Sweetheart, you don't make it easy. I didn't want to scare you off." He traced the delicate planes of her face with his fingertips, trailed by his lips. He kissed the outer corners of her eyes and along the sides of her nose. He kept his kisses and caresses light, not wanting her to draw away.

Her hands on him told him he needn't have worried.

She pressed butterfly kisses against his jaw and along the corners of his mouth. She was so engrossed in tasting him she didn't notice her nightgown rising up her legs until she felt his hand trailing a path up her calf.

"I don't look the way I did the last time," she murmured, reaching down to stop his hand.

He smiled. "I already figured that out." He rolled away long enough to pull off his T-shirt and shorts. When he finished, he still wore a pair of brightly colored boxers. He paused, looking questioningly at Gail as he held on to the hem of her nightgown. She smiled and nodded. Her nightgown soon drifted down to cover his clothing.

Gail wasn't the first naked pregnant woman he'd seen. He'd even delivered a few babies in the past. But she was the first woman who was pregnant because of him. Her breasts were much fuller, delicate veins tracing blue lines against her pale skin. And her belly was round with his child. He felt a wave of emotion wash over him as he caressed her, feeling the soft thumps of the baby within.

"My little one," he murmured, kissing the taut skin.

Gail bent her head over his, wrapping her arms around him.

Brian stretched out beside her, still keeping his arms around her. He wanted to take his time in reacquainting himself with her body. When he cupped her breasts, she moaned her appreciation. With every caress, she moved against him, mirroring it with one of her own.

Words were soft-spoken, filled with aching meaning as they explored each other's bodies. Under Brian's encouragement, Gail learned what aroused him. What had him whispering her name as a prayer and what had him moaning her name as a plea.

She swept her kisses across the hairy roughness of his chest and up to the sandpapery surface of his jaw. None of the textures of Brian were smooth until she encountered the part of him that was silken and steel.

"Oh my," she murmured, encircling him with her fingers. "Pure trouble."

"You're the pure trouble," he corrected, sliding his fingers into her and finding her moist and receptive. She clutched at him and arched up under his touch. He laid his hand on her belly. "I don't want to hurt you."

"You won't," she assured him. Her eyes were bright with desire as she guided him into her.

Brian hissed as she closed tightly around him. He wanted to be gentle with her. He wanted to take his time and give her as much pleasure as he could.

He wanted this to be a night that would never end.

It felt so right. *She* felt so right.

"Brian." His name was a whisper on her lips as she reached up to touch his face. The look of wonder on her face told him all he needed to know.

Nothing could be as perfect as it was this moment.

GAIL WAS FLOATING. First she'd felt as if she'd been shot out of a cannon into a world of colors then she floated downward on a soft fluffy cloud. She smiled. For someone who was confident she had no imagination, she was sure dreaming now.

She would have thought it was a dream if it wasn't for the warm male body lying spoon fashion behind her. His arm was draped over her waist, his hand possessive against her belly.

"Do you think he knows what we did?" he whispered, his lips brushing against her ear.

"I'm sure she pretended not to notice." She couldn't stop smiling. Why had she held him off for so long? The memory of their first time was nothing compared to what just happened.

"You're going to feel pretty silly when he comes out with a personality problem because you always called him a her," he said, rubbing lazy circles across her abdomen.

"You'll feel silly when she's born and you're looking for extra equipment and it's not there."

Brian levered himself up on his elbow so he could see her face. "You made a joke. The lady who likes everything in its place made a joke."

She slanted a sly look in his direction. "Must be the company I'm keeping."

"Wow, I am impressed. Before you know it, you'll be slipping whoopee cushions under the seats."

She took his hand and laced her fingers through it. "Not my style. But I'd suggest you be more careful from now on when you open cans of peanuts."

Brian couldn't keep back the burst of laughter that erupted from his chest. He rolled over onto his back and brought Gail with him. She lay sprawled on his chest.

"I've created a monster."

She smiled and shook her head. She cupped his face with her palms and kissed him gently. But even that started the flames flickering again.

"You created a woman," she softly corrected.

MUCH LATER, they lay quietly in a mutual afterglow. It took a moment for the soft sound to reach their ears.

Gail raised herself up and looked over the side of the bed. "Not tonight," she whispered.

"The guy has to go out?" Brian said sleepily. He rolled over and glanced at the clock. "Whoa, I hope he didn't have an accident somewhere."

"He can't help it. He's a puppy."

Brian climbed out of bed. He picked up his boxers and Gail's nightgown. The latter he laid on the bed behind him.

"I'll put him outside," he told her. "Want anything?"

"Cheese crackers and peanut butter. A glass of water, too. Please." She offered him a beaming smile.

"You're going to eat crackers in bed?"

Gail nodded. "I was never allowed to eat in bed. Not even when I was sick. I'm going to smother those crackers with peanut butter then I'm going to eat them. And if you're good—" her expression told him just how good she hoped he'd be "—I'll share with you."

Brian snatched up Duffy on the way to the door. "I'll be back before you know it." He paused as he reached the door. "And Gail? Duffy doesn't need to sleep with us tonight, does he? Like he's been sleeping with you every night? Something else I bet you wouldn't have been allowed to do."

He whistled merrily as he led Duffy outside and let him out on the grass. The puppy happily ran off to inspect the bushes.

Brian slouched in one of the chairs watching the puppy explore the yard. He should have been tired. Sleep wasn't something he'd been getting a lot of lately. Even at the station, he had trouble sleeping as he worried about Gail. And today hadn't ended up to be relaxing. Now that he'd briefly met Gail's parents he could better understand why she emotionally held herself back. He doubted there was a speck of emotion between the couple.

Irene and Patrick Roberts may have been married, but their body language spoke of two separate entities. Anyone not knowing them would have assumed they were two strangers who merely happened to arrive at the same time. There was no doubt they weren't all that impressed with Brian, but they didn't even band together then. Brian was proud of Gail for standing up to them. He wasn't sure if she'd done that too much in the past. But here she stood up for him. Made him feel damn good.

He was also thankful his parents and grandparents showed up when they did. They gave Gail's parents an excellent excuse to leave and Gail a chance to relax again. He was glad the Roberts were present to see his family warmly greet their daughter. Let them find out there were people who appreciated Gail for the person she was. Let them find out she had a man in her life. A man who loved her.

Brian shot up in his chair. Whoa. He'd used the *L* word and that was something he didn't use except among his family. But damn, he did love Gail.

She was prickly. Got a little too uptight at times. Really needed to work more on her sense of humor. But, man, she was definitely a diamond of first quality. He'd been telling himself it was a strong attraction and naturally, he would do the right thing by his child. And he'd even thought of a long-term relationship. Now he knew the long-term relationship involved even more. A ring. A church. All the trappings.

Duffy scampered up to him and whined.

Brian picked him up and scratched between his ears. The dog wiggled happily under the attention.

"She thinks I'll be leaving after the baby's born," he told the puppy. "I guess I'll have to prove to her that I'm here for good. She needs both of us, boy."

The puppy whimpered and tried to lick his face.

Brian coaxed Duffy into the laundry room and into his basket. The puppy didn't look happy, but he settled down in his blanket and closed his eyes.

Brian grabbed the items Gail had asked for and headed down the hallway.

"There's still some cake left," he told her as he cleared her nightstand and set down the pitcher of water, peanut butter jar and box of crackers.

"I'll have some for breakfast," she replied. "Unless you want to get me a chocolate doughnut." She flashed him a smile filled with seduction.

"There are no candy bars in my room. Since that night I'm not keeping any chocolate on the premises." He picked up the pitcher of ice water and poured a glass for each of them. He handed her one of them. "Of course, if you'd like to go a little further on convincing me you need chocolate, I'd be willing to reconsider," he said with a leer. He climbed back onto the empty side of the bed and leaned back against the headboard.

"The end result isn't worth it. But I will expect a huge hot fudge sundae after the baby is born," she told him. She daintily spread peanut butter on a cracker and handed it to him. She repeated her action with another cracker, this time nibbling on it.

He noticed a speck of peanut butter on her bottom lip. He leaned over and captured it with his tongue. He looked into her face, enjoying the blush coloring her cheeks. "Tastes better on you than on the cracker."

Not taking her eyes off him, she picked up the peanut butter jar and scooped out a bit on her finger. She dabbed it gently on his lower lip then leaned over and flicked it off with her tongue.

"Hmm, I'd have to say that it tastes much better on you," she murmured. She half turned away, reaching for the peanut butter jar again. "Maybe I should double-check that—" Her hand was snatched up and she was spun back around. She uttered a surprised laugh as he pulled her down on top of him. She wiggled herself into a more comfortable position that elicited another response from Brian. Her eyes widened.

"I can't help it. I'm making up for lost time." He cupped the back of her head and brought her face down to his. Gail merely smiled and gave herself up to him.

GAIL FELT as comfortable as if she were snuggling up with a warm quilt. Except this quilt had a heartbeat. She lay still, savoring the warmth surrounding her. She ran a mental catalog. Brian's arms wrapped around her. His lips against her temple, his breath warm against her skin. His legs lay tangled with hers. They were as close as they had been when they made love. The thought sent warm tingles through her body. Tingles that were quickly increasing.

Then she felt it.

Something warm and damp against her leg.

Not identifiable at first.

"Brian?" she whispered.

"Yeah?" His voice was sleepy and sounding all too self-satisfied.

He was on the wrong side for the warm and damp against her leg. She gingerly shifted it. Warm and fuzzy.

She lifted her head and looked down the length of the bed. A tan-and-black head lifted upward, a wet nose twitching as Duffy happily wiggled among the covers.

"How did you?"

"Do you know he'll just sit there and cry until you put him on the bed?" Brian said in her ear. "I guess he figured since he's been sleeping with you all along, he shouldn't be left out now."

Busted!

"He'd look up at me with these big brown eyes," Gail confessed.

"What about big blue eyes?" he asked. "They have a chance, too?"

She pretended to consider his words. "Well, it was those blue eyes that first got my attention. And you are better than a blanket." She slid back into his arms.

Brian looked down at Duffy who was watching them with avid curiosity.

"Fella, there are some things you just don't need to know."

GAIL WALKED through the bedroom, mentally repainting walls, changing curtains and adding new furniture.

"I need to clean out and start fresh," she told herself.

"Start fresh with what?" Brian came in. He slid his arms around her waist and pulled her back against him. He nuzzled the side of her neck.

She placed her hands on his locked hands. "What is supposed to be the nursery."

"Well, no wonder you were willing to let me move into your bedroom. You were going to kick me out of here anyway." He lifted his head, now resting his chin against her hair. "I can call my brothers and we can have the furniture moved out in no time. Do you want to store it?"

She shook her head. "If you know someone who needs a bedroom suite, it's theirs." She turned around in his arms. She placed her palms against his chest, moving them upward to loop around his neck. "I want to go to a paint store. I want to do all of this myself."

"You won't be doing any painting," Brian informed her. "I'll do all the heavy work and you'll supervise."

"Teddy bears. Soft pastels. Maybe carousels," she mused.

He released her and spun around, clutching his head with his hands. "Teddy bears and pastels? For a boy? Not a good idea, Gail! He'll be teased by all the other boy babies for having a sissy room! Why not race cars or a train theme? Dinosaurs. Guy stuff? The kind of stuff he can be proud of when other babies come over to play."

Gail shook her head. "There's only one thing to do. Wait until the sonogram. I have that next week and we'll find out the sex of the baby then. Until then, we'll just concentrate on clearing out the room and choosing paint for the walls. I'd rather use a neutral color anyway. Wallpaper can wait until later." She patted his shoulders and moved away. "I'll take a shower and get dressed, so we can go out to the paint store today. Maybe we'll have time to look at baby furniture, too."

"When you're ready to do something, you don't waste any time, do you?" Brian gathered up clean clothing. He had an idea if he wasn't ready on time, Gail would go without him!

Before they left, Brian pointed out neither of their cars were appropriate for the kind of shopping they were planning to do. He made a call to Jeff and they stopped off at his brother's place swapping Brian's Corvette for Jeff's Cherokee.

"Don't worry, little bro, I'll take good care of it." Jeff grinned as Brian helped Gail into the passenger seat.

Brian noticed Gail had no idea what to do the moment she entered the huge home center. He guided her toward the rear of the building where the paints were displayed. Gail stood in front of the large array of paint sample cards, picking up several, then putting down others. Since Brian didn't see how important the color of the walls could be, he stayed behind her and nodded at whatever she said.

"I don't want anything beige," she murmured. "A cream is nice. Or even this seashell. Hmm, wouldn't this sea mint be pretty in my bathroom?" She held up a sample. She shook her head. "No, I have to worry about the nursery first." But she tucked the mint sample card in her purse.

"Who knew there would be so many shades of cream," he remarked, grabbing a sample and holding it up. "Why can't we just paint the walls white? Everything goes with white."

Gail stared at him as if he'd lost his mind.

"Not a good idea, I guess," he mumbled.

"White is much too stark." She searched through the samples again. When she turned to him, she stared at the sample card in his hand. "This is perfect!" She snatched it out of his hand as she looked around for a sales clerk. "How much do you think we'll need?"

"Finally, I'm necessary."

After an argument over who would pay for the paint and supplies, which Brian won, they left the center. Brian quickly stored them in the back of the Jeep.

"There's some baby stores nearby," Gail told him.

"Lunch first," he insisted. He held up his hand to stall off her protest. "Maybe you don't think you're hungry, but I am."

If he thought they'd relax during their meal, he was quickly proven wrong.

After they ordered their food, Gail pulled out a notebook and began writing.

"A crib, a changing table, a chest of drawers, diaper pail, a playpen," she said as she wrote.

"What about one of those swing things? Abby and Jeff's girls loved theirs," he suggested.

"And we'll have to childproof the house. Covers for outlets, locks for cabinet doors. May as well start doing it early."

He wondered if she realized she'd said *we* instead of *I*. Definitely a point for his side.

"You don't need to find it all today," Brian said as he dug into his hamburger. "The room will have to be cleaned out and painted first. And you've got your work, too."

Gail shook her head. "I'm only working until the end of the month. Then I'll start my maternity leave."

"You'll go crazy with so much time on your hands."

"No, I'll have time to sit back and relax." She tore bits off the bun of her chicken sandwich.

Brian popped a French fry into his mouth. "I put in for paternity leave, too." He shook his head when she opened her mouth. "I intend to be around twenty-four/seven until the baby is born. No arguments."

"All right." She leaned over and stole a fry from his plate.

Brian eyed her warily. "You agreed awfully fast."

Gail shrugged. "Why waste my time arguing?" She grabbed another fry and bit into it. "You feel you need to do it."

"You got it." He moved his plate further away from her. She made a face.

"I only wanted a few."

"And you've had them."

"I'd like to see you go through a pregnancy," she challenged. "One bout of morning sickness and you'd be ready to give it back."

"You got it, honey," the waitress cheered as she set down another glass of Coke for Brian. "And once you're in labor, they're turning green and passing out cold. Or down at the corner bar for a drink telling everyone what a great man they are." She eyed Brian. "You stay with her, hon. Don't be like my ex."

"I intend to be with the little lady all the way," he vowed with a rogue's grin.

She patted his shoulder as she left.

"Little lady?" Gail repeated. "My nausea might be under control now, but there's no reason to push it."

After they finished their lunch, Gail suggested they walk to the first store since it was only a few doors down. She'd barely entered the store when she wanted to leave.

"What's wrong? Are you feeling okay?" he asked.

She shook her head. "I'm fine. I can't say why. I just didn't feel right in there." She checked the list she'd made out. "I guess we'll have to drive to the next store. It's at the mall."

"THIS IS IT." Gail ran her hand lightly across the smooth surface of the wood. "It's perfect."

Brian glanced at the price tag and gulped. "Perfect if you plan on having ten kids. I don't think I paid this much for all my bedroom furniture."

"This isn't bad at all." She dismissed the price. "Let's see what else they have." She moved off toward the rear of the store.

Brian watched Gail, realizing this was another side to her. He'd heard pregnant women go into a nesting stage near the end of their pregnancy. Gail's just started a little early. She had a couple months until the baby was due so he was surprised she was taking time off early. He knew how much she cared about her work.

But now she has something else to think about. And she was going to do her best for this child.

Well, so was he.

Chapter Fifteen

"It's not the same."

"It's the same."

"No, it's not. It's darker."

"Dammit, Gail, it is not darker! Don't forget you're looking at the wall, not the stupid sample! And the paint hasn't dried yet."

Gail pulled the paint sample chip out of her pocket and walked over to the wall that was half painted. She laid it next to the painted section.

"Told you it was the same," Brian said looking to his brothers for support.

Jeff and Mark who stood at opposite walls took one look at Gail's set features and wisely remained silent.

"Cowards," Brian muttered.

Gail pulled back the sample. "It's still a bit darker, but I guess there's nothing we can do about it." She glanced at Jeff and Mark. "Is there a problem?"

"Nope, not a one," Jeff intoned.

"Everything's fine by me. It's a bit darker, but it will do," Mark ducked his head, turning back to the section of wall he was painting.

Gail stared at each of them then turned on her heel and stalked out of the room.

"Wimps," Brian growled, glaring at his brothers.

"Self-preservation," Jeff made his excuse.

Mark nodded. "I thought PMS was bad, but pregnancy really turns a woman into something inhuman," he said with quiet awe. "It's almost enough to turn a man celibate." His two brothers looked at him as if he'd uttered the most ridiculous statement in history. Especially since Mark was known to have a new girlfriend every month. "I said *almost* enough."

"He'll never change," Jeff told Brian.

"That room needs to be finished by tonight so it will be thoroughly dry by the time the furniture arrives tomorrow afternoon!" Gail shouted from the other side of the house.

"Next time you call me up and ask if I can help you out?" Jeff said, dipping his roller into the paint-filled tray. *"Don't."*

Brian quickly returned to his own work. "Gotcha."

Luckily, the men finished their work in plenty of time. Since the evening was warm enough, Brian opened the windows.

"You're right. It looks darker than the sample because it's wet," Mark said, holding the paint sample card against the wall.

"I don't think that will fly with Gail," Brian said.

Gail appeared in the doorway. "It still looks darker."

Wisely, none of the men said anything.

BY MORNING, Gail commented the walls looked exactly the way they should. Brian could only heave a silent sigh of relief. That turned into a groan when the nursery furniture arrived.

"Perhaps we should have wallpapered one wall," she mused, as he put the mobile together and attached it to the top of the crib. "Or added a border. I saw one of circus animals that was darling. That wouldn't be difficult to put up, would it?" She tested the wall surface with her fingertip.

"Gail, honey, the baby isn't arriving tomorrow, so you don't need to make the decision right now," he said.

"But everything needs to be ready." She walked around, her fingertips trailing over each piece of furniture. She stopped at the rocking chair and with a flick of her fingers sent it gently bobbing back and forth.

Brian pulled her over to him and wrapped his arms around her. She tried to shrug him away, but he merely tightened his hold.

"You can't even get your arms around me," she muttered, dipping her head.

"This is better. I can feel the baby rolling around. Tonight must be his bowling night." He nuzzled the side of her neck. "Mmm, you smell so sexy. You always smell sexy, but you smell even sexier tonight."

She placed her hands over his. "It's getting close."

He wiggled his hips against her. "I'm trying."

"Brian!"

"Everything will be fine." He turned her around and kissed her. Then kissed her again. "Think that crib would hold us?"

Gail laughed and shook her head as she rested her forehead against his chest.

SHE COULDN'T SLEEP. She should have been able to. It had been a busy day working in the nursery and making sure everything was right. She was pleasantly tired, and now she lay curled up next to Brian who was comfortably sprawled next to her. Soft snuffling sounds emitted from his lips. Duffy slept heavily on her feet. She dreaded to think what would happen when the dog reached his full growth. She doubted even her king-size bed would fit all three of them.

There it was again. Thinking of them as long-term.

She carefully edged herself away from Brian and slipped out of bed. She picked up the shawl Martha had knitted for her and wrapped it around her shoulders. Duffy raised his head then scrambled off the bed to follow her.

The night-light burning in the hallway allowed her to make her way into the room that now smelled new to her. The moonlight spilling through the open blinds lent ghostly shapes to the furniture. She walked over to the rocking chair and sat down. Out of habit, she started to curl her legs up under her until she realized her unwieldy shape wouldn't allow it. She settled for keeping her feet on the floor. Duffy loped over and immediately dropped on top of her feet. He gave a jaw-breaking yawn and promptly fell back asleep.

She looked around the room. The walls were still blank. So far she hadn't found pictures for them. She wanted something as warm as the rest of the room.

She pictured how the room would look when the baby would be sleeping peacefully in the crib or she sitting here nursing her. Maybe Brian would be awake and come in with her. They would talk softly about things they wouldn't have thought of during the day. Future dreams for their child.

She was doing it again. Thinking of him as long-term.

Gail was afraid of long-term. She didn't want the kind of cold, loveless marriage her parents seemed to enjoy. If *enjoy* was a word in their vocabulary.

She'd never known a man who was as open and warm as Brian. He hadn't blamed her for the pregnancy as some men would have done. He hadn't even suggested the unthinkable or implied the baby might not have been his. He'd merely done what he felt was right. He was there for her. Even his family had welcomed her without reservation. Something her parents would never have done.

Now she was scared. So scared she was falling in love with Brian. Scared she wouldn't be able to give him the love he deserved. The kind of love she might not have inside her. She placed her hands against her abdomen. The baby was quiet, so she guessed she was sleeping even if her mother couldn't.

She wrapped the shawl tightly around her as if she were cold. Except the cold couldn't be swept away by covering herself. Not when it was so deeply embedded inside her.

"WHERE HAVE YOU BEEN?" Gail demanded in a voice that almost shrieked hysteria.

"I had to run an errand," Brian explained, sauntering into her bedroom as if he had all the time in the world.

"An errand? You ran some lousy errand when you knew what time we had to leave here?" She ran her brush through her hair then tossed it onto the bed. A clear sign she was agitated since she never left things where they didn't belong.

He shrugged. "I knew I'd be back in plenty of time before your appointment." He glanced toward the clock by the bed. "And I was."

"Well, good for you for being on time. As you said, my appointment. I hate tests," she grumbled, rummaging through her closet. She pulled several outfits out and put them back. She held up a bright-pink cotton dress. "Why did I buy this? I look like a bag of cotton candy in it.'' She pushed it back into her closet. 'Where did you go?''

Brian sat on the edge of the bed. He jammed his hands in his pockets as he watched her tear her closet apart.

''I had to pick something up. Why are you so worried about what to wear? Is there a dress code or something? There's nothing invasive about a sonogram, so there's nothing to worry about,'' he said helpfully. ''They're just going to take pictures of the baby.''

She whirled on him. ''It's still a test, dammit!''

Since Gail rarely swore, Brian knew how nervous she was.

''Honey, there's nothing to be afraid of,'' he soothed. ''You're not worried they'll tell you you're having twins, are you? Or triplets or—''

''If you don't shut up, you will not go with me.''

He knew when to shut up and this was the time.

''I'll make sure Duffy is taken care of,'' he said, taking his leave.

Gail rubbed her forehead with her fingertips. She knew on a logical side there was no reason to be nervous of the sonogram. She was a doctor and had seen it performed many times. But from the beginning, she'd found things to worry about. As a doctor, she could calm her patient's fears, explain why a procedure was necessary. As a patient, she might know what was going to happen, but it still didn't make things any easier.

Maybe it was routine. Maybe it was a test that was done every day. But it wasn't done every day on her! This had to do with her baby's health and well-being. What if they found something wrong?

Her hands shook as she pulled out a dress and slipped it on.

She silently insisted there couldn't be anything wrong

with the baby. She would know if there was. She would sense it. She continually reminded herself of that fact as she finished getting ready.

When she finished, she walked out into the family room where Brian was sitting on the floor playing tug-of-war with Duffy.

"You're getting dog hair all over you!" she shrieked.

"He's got short hair, Gail." He stood up and brushed off his shorts. "Ready?"

"No."

HE TOOK ONE LOOK at her face and walked over to her. He bent his head and kissed her leisurely as if he had all the time in the world. When he stepped back, they were both breathless.

"After your appointment, you're going to buy the kid a football," he said, as they walked outside.

"Don't hold your breath." She stopped short at the sight of the sage-green Cherokee standing in the driveway. "What is this?"

"Can't put a baby seat in the 'Vette." He disarmed the alarm and opened the passenger door.

As Gail climbed in, she noticed a baby seat already installed in the back.

"But your car," she babbled, twisting around in her seat as Brian climbed in behind the wheel. "You love that car. It's a known fact men think more of their cars than anything else."

He had started the ignition but shut it off and turned to face her. "Gail, it's just a car. One that required a lot of TLC and I had to borrow either my dad's or one of my brothers' trucks when I had to haul anything."

She shook her head, unable to believe it all. Brian

muttered a curse. He flicked off his seat belt, so he could better face her. He grasped her face between his hands.

"What's important is a safe place for the baby," he stated. "Besides, this baby is four-wheel drive. Think what we can do on weekends." He grinned and kissed her. "The seats are pretty comfy if you want to try them out," he murmured. "How about it? A quickie before we go?"

Gail laughed. "Out here in the driveway where the neighbors would see?"

"Sure, give them something to talk about." He checked her seat belt before fastening his own. "Okay, but it's your loss. Not to mention mine," he muttered forlornly, as he started up the car.

As Brian drove he extolled the virtues of the sports utility vehicle showing off its abilities the way a kid showed off his new toy. By the time they reached the medical center parking lot, Gail knew as much about the truck as Brian did.

"I'll take you out so you can practice driving it," he told her, as they walked into the building.

"I know how to drive," she said dryly.

"A car, yes. This isn't like driving a car."

"How macho," she murmured, heading down the hallway.

Brian lagged behind her, enjoying the sight.

"Did you know you sorta waddle?"

Gail stopped short and spun around. Her expression could have stripped paint.

"I *what?*" Her voice was dangerously soft.

He had no idea how much danger he was courting. "Waddle. I guess it's because your weight is basically up front."

Gail held up her hand in a "stop" motion. "If you

value your life, you will not say another word." She spun back around and grabbed the door handle. She flung the door open with more force than necessary.

"What did I say?" He was bewildered as he followed her inside.

Gail wasn't about to tell Brian his less than tactful remark took her mind off the upcoming procedure.

By the time the technician started the sonogram, she was torn between debating whether she would speak to Brian again or worrying about the baby.

"There we are," the technician announced.

Gail's head whipped around so she could view the monitor. "Oh, my God," she whispered. Tears filled her eyes as she gazed at the tiny being nestled deep within her.

"Wow," Brian breathed, leaning in for a closer look. "He's on his side, isn't he? Looking at us."

Gail laughed, the sound fuller and richer than it had been in a long time. A sound free of worry as she saw the child she already deemed perfect.

"She," the technician corrected.

He straightened up. "She?" He glanced at Gail who shot him a told-you-so look.

"You're going to have a little girl." The technician pushed a button and a photo slid out. He handed it to Gail. "I'd say she's going to have your looks."

Brian puffed up. "Damn straight."

They walked out of the medical center, heads bent as they studied the photo of their baby.

"She's so much more real to me," Gail whispered around a throat full of tears.

He helped her into the Cherokee. "And beautiful."

He didn't start up the truck right away as they continued looking at the photo. Gail lifted her head and turned to Brian. Her brown eyes shimmered with tears. She reached out and touched his cheek. She turned her hand around, staring at her damp fingertips.

"Guys can cry, too," he told her in a low voice. He grasped her fingers and kissed each one. He kept her hand in his, placing it on his thigh as he started up the truck.

The silence that followed wasn't comfortable as Brian drove. He stopped at a fast-food restaurant, grabbed some drinks and something to eat, and drove to a nearby park. He carried their food and drinks to a table where he sat next to Gail.

"A lot has happened these past months," he said slowly, as he handed her a small cinnamon bun and her juice. "I've gotten to know you better. Your prickly side and your soft side." He smiled. "We have a baby coming. We're living together and do pretty well. I want the baby to have my name. Not just on the birth certificate. But on everything."

Gail's hand froze so that her cup of juice rested against her lips. She set it down carefully, as if fearing she would spill the contents. Her fingers were braced alongside the cup. Her gaze focused on the cup as she spoke.

"She will have your name."

"What about you?"

She exhaled a deep breath.

"Okay, not exactly the place for a proposal." Brian looked off toward the playground that was filled with small children. He thought of his daughter playing over there in a few years. He used to think his schedule was crazy. Now he was glad he would have days free he could spend with his child. "But the feeling's there." He covered her hand with his. He wanted to tell her he loved her, but something held him back. Crazy, he knew. After all, doesn't a man tell a woman he loves her when he asks her to marry him? But he wasn't sure she'd believe him. "We're a well-rounded medical family. In many ways I have a flexible schedule so there would be days I'd be home with the baby. You'd talked about cutting back on your hours, so we could easily share the care."

"I need to think about this," she whispered. She looked up, locking her gaze with his. "Please?"

"Don't want to fly to Las Vegas right now?" he joked, sensing a lessening of tension was needed.

She managed a weak smile but said nothing.

"We're great together even if you do go more than a little ballistic when it comes to chocolate." Brian dunked his cinnamon bun in the vanilla icing and popped it into his mouth followed by a swallow of coffee.

Gail finished her juice in several swallows and got up, dropping the cup in the trash can.

"Could we look for pictures for the nursery?" she asked. "The walls really need something."

He nodded. "Sure. We'll go anywhere you want."

As they walked toward the waiting truck, Gail knew that the subject was far from finished. Brian was like a terrier who refused to let something go. He wasn't going to let her forget he'd asked her to marry him.

Her first proposal. Not what she'd expected or thought she'd hear when a man asked her to marry her. No soft music, candlelight or even a hovering waiter. There was one more important thing missing.

He hadn't said he loved her.

Chapter Sixteen

Just before Gail opened the door to the center, she stopped for a moment.

"Second thoughts?" Brian asked quietly.

She shook her head. "I need the time home to get ready." She took a deep breath and pushed open the door.

Sheila was coming out of the coffee room when Gail and Brian walked in.

"You've got a very light day today," she announced, hugging Gail then hugging Brian. "Hey handsome, care to help me pull something down from a shelf?"

"Sure," he followed her into the coffee room.

"Lora's got some messages for you out front," Sheila told Gail.

Gail rubbed the small of her back as she walked down the hallway.

"Quack quack," Brian called after her. He laughed at her retort. "Hey! That's not the kind of gesture a future mother should use."

"Then don't provoke this future mother," she snapped back as she headed for the front desk.

When Gail reached the reception area, she noticed the room was still dim.

"Lora," she called out.

As she crossed the threshold, the lights suddenly blazed on causing her to blink against the brightness.

"Surprise!"

Gail stared at the room filled with children, their parents and her colleagues, all wearing party hats. A large sheet cake decorated with pink frosting dominated a table. Another table was piled high with wrapped gifts.

"Did we surprise you, Dr. Gail?" One young boy ran up to her and hopped up and down with excitement. "Did we?"

She nodded as she leaned down to hug him. "Yes, you did, Joel. You all surprised me a lot."

"Joel and I overheard the nurses talk about a surprise shower for you and we asked if we could be included," the boy's mother explained. She gestured to the crowd behind her. "As you can see, a lot of the other mothers wanted to get involved, too."

Gail tried to speak but the emotion flooding her senses wouldn't allow words to come forth. She was barely aware of the handkerchief thrust into her hand or of Brian's arm around her shoulders.

"Ladies, I have to say this surprise is much better than the one the guys down at the fire station gave me," he said easily, keeping Gail by his side as he guided her to the chair that was designated for her. He kissed her lightly on the lips. "I'll be back later," he told her. "Have fun."

"Most definitely the first baby shower that kids wanted input," Sheila said as Gail unwrapped gifts. "You'd be amazed how many suggested an ice-cream cake."

Gail looked over at the corner set up with small tables and chairs and toys for the patients. Now, plates of cake and cups of punch littered the tabletops. She was touched her young patients wanted to help surprise her.

"YOU REALLY hauled it in," Brian commented. He paused to admire the stroller designed for the serious runner who wanted to take the baby along. "This is cool. I can take Miss Junior out for a run."

Gail smiled as she held up a pale-pink sleeper embroidered with tiny bunnies. "Isn't this adorable? Lora gave us this."

"Not my color," he admitted. "But the baby will love it."

"I can't believe they did all this." She gestured toward the table, which still held half a cake. Brian wasted no time in going over and cutting himself a piece. "And so many of my patients came." When she looked up at him, her face was flushed with color, and her eyes sparkled with excitement. She pointed out various gifts and explained who brought them.

What Brian noticed touched her the most were hand-drawn and colored pictures or baby cards from some of her patients. Many of them showing a lopsided baby sleeping in a crib or cradle.

"Come back soon, Doctor Gail."

"I love you, Doctor Gail."

"I had no idea," she murmured.

"That's what I love about you, Doc." Brian dropped a kiss on the top of her head. "You're completely oblivious to how wonderful you are."

Gail's face snapped upward. "You never said that before," she whispered.

He frowned for a moment as if not understanding what she was getting at. Then his expression cleared.

"Maybe I did and you just weren't listening," he

whispered back, this time kissing her on the lips. "Personally, I think you're pretty hot stuff."

"My hormones are crazy enough, thank you very much," she said primly. "If you aren't careful, you'll be attacked by a crazed pregnant woman once we get home."

He grinned. "Don't worry, I can handle it."

Predictably, Gail cried as she said her goodbyes. Brian and Ted loaded the truck with the gifts as she alternately sobbed and hugged everyone.

"Hey, no waterfalls, you'll be back," Ted assured her with a bear hug. "Just don't worry about anything. We'll take good care of your patients while you're gone. And you take good care of her." He looked at Brian.

"I will," he promised, helping her into the passenger seat then handing her his handkerchief.

By the time they reached the house, Gail was starting to feel more like herself.

As Brian unpacked the truck, she again pointed out each gift and explained who gave it to her. She personally carried in the baby snow globe night-light Sheila had given her. She placed it on the chest of drawers and plugged it in.

Gail looked around, pleased with the pictures of babies dressed up as flowers that now dotted the walls. She'd found wallpaper border in colors that matched the pictures. Brian obligingly put it up one weekend.

"Add one baby and it's finished," she murmured.

"My little one," Brian said, standing behind her. He wrapped his arms around her middle.

She leaned back in his arms, content to just stay there.

He said he loved her. Said it in front of others. Then he said he'd been saying it all along and she just wasn't listening.

Was that it?

He'd asked her to marry him. Would Brian have done that just to do the right thing or because he truly wanted to marry her? She knew he wouldn't ask her again. It would be up to her next.

She knew she spent too much time trying to figure things out. It was a habit of hers.

The only spontaneous thing she'd ever done was call him to be her date.

Funny thing was, it turned out to be the best thing she'd ever done.

TIME WAS GETTING SHORT. Brian felt it as if a storm were coming. In a way, one was. Except this one would be in human form.

The house was so clean it was practically sterile. Gail had cleaned out her closet and got rid of the conservative clothing she used to be so fond of. She'd seen Ginna again and this time, got her hair cut a little shorter. At first, she cried claiming it was too short, then the next day she decided she loved it.

His parents stopped by with a baby quilt Cathy had made from scraps of Brian's clothing. Gail clutched it to her chest and cried.

For a woman who rarely used to show emotion, she was sure doing a lot of it now.

She even cried at dog food commercials.

She waddled even more, and she complained she hadn't seen her feet in ages.

All it did was make him love her more.

He just wished she'd finally wake up and realize how much he loved her so they could get married and get this show on the road!

He wanted them married before she had the baby. He

didn't mention it again because he wasn't sure if it was a good idea. But time was getting short, so it looked as though he was going to have to do something about it.

Maybe he should just toss her over his shoulder and carry her off to Las Vegas. His family would help. He'd have to let them in on it or they'd never forgive him.

He'd even gone so far as to ask his dad and brothers while they repaired the fence on Cathy and Lou's property. His dad had called early the night before and asked Brian over to help out. With Gail so close to her due date, Brian had taken his pager with him and made her promise to call if she even had a twinge.

"Why not stay for dinner," Cathy suggested. "I talked Gail into taking a nap, so you'd even have time to shower."

"I didn't exactly bring a change of clothes with me."

"I'm sure we can find something for you to wear." She pushed him down the hallway toward his old bedroom.

Brian dragged himself into the bathroom and turned on the shower. He thought of all the stories of first babies coming early and in the middle of the night. "Stay put tonight, okay, little one?" he said out loud. "Daddy really needs his sleep."

After his shower, he dried off and briefly thought of just asking if he and Gail could spend the night there. They wouldn't need to worry about Duffy since they'd brought the puppy with them. He knotted the towel around his waist and returned to his bedroom where he knew his mother would have laid out some clothes for him.

He was surprised to find not only clothing lying across his old bed but also Gail, now dressed in a cream lace gown, seated on the bed.

"You look beautiful," he told her. "I'm just glad you didn't see me when I was covered with dirt and sweat."

Her expression was solemn when she looked up.

"Brian Walker, will you marry me?"

He sat down before his legs gave out on him. He grabbed his towel before it could part company with his body. He felt this was not a moment to be naked.

"Could you run that by me again? I think I got some water in my ear."

"I asked you to marry me. Before, you'd asked me, but I knew I wasn't ready. I didn't want our marriage to be one of convenience because of the baby," she said quietly. "I was also afraid I wouldn't be able to give you what you deserved. I didn't know if I had it within me. Bit by bit, you seemed to have chipped away that barrier and with it gone, I learned that I did have it. I had it all along. I just needed someone to show me where it was. And you were that person. So I'm asking you if you would do me the honor of becoming my husband and the father of our baby."

He wasn't giving her a chance to reconsider what she said. "Yes."

The smile came and went on her lips. She carefully stood up. "Then I suggest you get ready for our wedding, so we won't be late."

"Our what?"

She gestured toward the window. "While your father kept you busy all day, the rest of us were busy here."

"Honey, we can't get married that fast. Blood tests, license and all that." He only wished they could!

She smirked. "Blood tests were no problem and if one of your patients happens to be the son of a judge, you can cut through a lot of red tape. So get changed and I'll meet you downstairs."

Brian took a quick look outside. A flower-covered bower had been set up with chairs facing it. Judging from the crowd out there, everyone knew about it but him. Even Duffy sported a large bow. Not wanting to wrinkle her gown, he kept his hands on her shoulders.

"You were that sure of me, were you?" he teased.

The smile she gave him was pure female. "Let's just say I was that sure of *me*."

He hated to settle for a quick kiss, but that was all right. He'd gladly wait for the rest.

THE WEDDING WAS everything a wedding should be. Especially a wedding planned by the Walker women who were determined to have a wedding to end all weddings. Brian's mother, grandmother and sisters cried. The male members of the family told him he was better off. Not that he needed to hear it. He only had to look at Gail, see the love fully shining on her face to know it.

Even Duffy howling as the minister spoke the words didn't matter. And everything was on video.

But it wasn't until the minister introduced them to the audience as husband and wife, that Brian knew Gail was truly his.

"I love you," he whispered as he kissed her amid the applause and whistles.

"And I love you," she whispered back. "Brian? Do you mind if we skip the reception?"

"Sounds fine to me." He wanted nothing more than to be alone with her.

"Good, because I've been in labor for the last two hours."

JENNIFER MARIE WALKER was born just a little after midnight at six pounds, two ounces. Her dad took one look at her and vowed she wouldn't date until she was thirty.

Her mom took one look at her and vowed to keep her daddy in line so she could have all the fun a girl should have.

* * * *

Look out for next month's **THAT'S MY BABY!** *story*—Daddy in Demand *by Muriel Jensen will be on the shelves in July 2002.*

SILHOUETTE
SPECIAL EDITION

AVAILABLE FROM 21ST JUNE 2002

DADDY IN DEMAND Muriel Jensen

That's My Baby!

When Dori McKeon found an abandoned baby she turned to estranged husband Sal Dominguez. Sal was happy to help solve the puzzle—and to try and win Dori back…this time—forever!

THE STRANGER IN ROOM 205 Gina Wilkins

Hot Off the Press

Instinct told newspaper owner Serena Schaffer that the injured man she'd found was not who he proclaimed to be. But one look into Sam's eyes and Serena was ready to believe anything…

WHEN I SEE YOUR FACE Laurie Paige

Windraven Legacy

Rory Daniels knew that if temporarily blinded Shannon Bannock could just find the courage to trust him, he could show her so much—he could show her forever…

STORMING WHITEHORN Christine Scott

Montana Brides

Storm Hunter had coldly refused Jasmine's charms. The chasm between their ages and cultures was too wide. But how could Storm continue to resist when the virginal beauty still looked at him that way?

STARTING WITH A KISS Barbara McMahon

When prim-and-proper Abigail Trent asked Dr Greg Hastings to help turn her into an irresistible temptress, she never thought that after just one kiss she would start to hope that Greg was her Prince Charming…

STRANGER IN A SMALL TOWN Ann Roth

B&B owner and single mum Alison O'Hara was like no woman loner Clint had ever met. Could she transform him into a husband—and a daddy to her little girl?

THE STANISLASKIS

NORA ROBERTS

The Stanislaski family saga continues in

Considering
Kate

A brand-new Silhouette Special Edition
title from multi-*New York Times*
bestselling author
Nora Roberts.

Available from 17th May 2002

0602/121/SH29

FREE
2 BOOKS
AND A SURPRISE GIFT!

We would like to take this opportunity to thank you for reading this Silhouette® book by offering you the chance to take TWO more specially selected titles from the Special Edition™ series absolutely FREE! We're also making this offer to introduce you to the benefits of the Reader Service™—

- ★ FREE home delivery
- ★ FREE monthly Newsletter
- ★ FREE gifts and competitions
- ★ Exclusive Reader Service discount
- ★ Books available before they're in the shops

Accepting these FREE books and gift places you under no obligation to buy; you may cancel at any time, even after receiving your free shipment. Simply complete your details below and return the entire page to the address below. **You don't even need a stamp!**

YES! Please send me 2 free Special Edition books and a surprise gift. I understand that unless you hear from me, I will receive 4 superb new titles every month for just £2.85 each, postage and packing free. I am under no obligation to purchase any books and may cancel my subscription at any time. The free books and gift will be mine to keep in any case.

EZZEC

Ms/Mrs/Miss/Mr ....Initials..................................
BLOCK CAPITALS PLEASE

Surname..

Address..

....

....Postcode ....

Send this whole page to:
UK: FREEPOST CN81, Croydon, CR9 3WZ
EIRE: PO Box 4546, Kilcock, County Kildare (stamp required)